CONTRITION

Book One of the Series,
Kelsey's Journey
Heather Vacca Voccola

Contrition
A Novel

Copyright © 2015 Heather Vacca Voccola
All rights reserved

Published by Goodbooks Media
Book design by James Ridley
Cover photo by Bill Kainer

Ad Majorem Dei Gloriam

Queries to
Heather Vacca Voccola
author@heathervoccola.com
mobile: 860.490.8314

ISBN-13: 978-1512058628
ISBN-10: 1512058629

goodbook

goodbooksmedia.com
3453 Aransas
Corpus Christi, Texas, 78411

Dedication

To my parents, Mom and Dayod,
who gave me life and love

To my daughters, Alyssa and Rebecca,
who gave my life true meaning

To my family, Frank, Kris and Angela,
who share my life

To my heroes, Stevie and Birgitta,
who love life every day

And to Saint John Paul II and Fr. Dennis,
who keep my life on the right road

Acknowledgements

This story has been a long time coming and so many people made it possible. I must first thank my parents for giving me life and a love of reading and writing. I thank my daughters who complained that there were not enough stories for Catholic teens and could I get on that. I thank Tom and April Hoopes and Fr. Owen Kearns for my very first paid writing opportunity. I thank Robyn Lee most importantly for being my friend, but also for finding me other writing opportunities over the years. Thanks also must go to Dr. Cynthia Toolin who introduced me to NaNoWriMo all those years ago and then joyfully read the product of it, which was very different than it is today.

Special thanks are reserved for Dr. Ronda Chervin, who spent hours with me and my manuscript in her little cell encouraging and guiding me through the editing process with Elizabeth Hanink, and then finding me a great publisher to work with. Thank you to James Ridley and Good Books Media for taking a chance on Catholic Young Adult fiction. Thank you, Danielle Bean and Patrick Madrid, for your kind words, prayers and enthusiasm.

There are so many other folks that need thanking for being friends that are like family: Fran & Jim, Dee-Dee & Charlie, Lynn & Tom, Susie, Misti and all of your respective children along with my four loves: Monica & Birgitta and June & Stevie. My work family: Fr. Check, Fr. Bochanski, and Angelo along with my HACS friends: Bob, Alicia, Alicia, Carol & Debra - you all make my days brighter. For Michelle who held my hand and pressed for answers to get me a fabulous looking website. For Allie who is and Dylan who isn't.

For the little baby whose thirteen year old mother I walked to the Abortion Mill back in my college days, I wish to ask for your forgiveness. I thought I was helping, but now I know better. I have never forgotten either of you. I hope this humble work stops someone from making that same mistake.

And finally for my prayer warriors - the Canons Regular of St. John Cantius, especially Fr. Dennis, Fr. Robin, Fr. Nathan, Fr. Joshua and Fr. Kevin. For the Fathers of Mercy, especially Fr. Ken, Fr. Andy, Fr. Ricardo, Fr. John and Fr. Tony. Also for Fr. Jeff and Fr. Dairo. And for Fr. Fluet, for introducing me to the beauty of Mass celebrated the way all Masses should be. Don't think that I don't know that the number of prayers you all have said on my behalf outnumber the stars in the sky. No words of thanks will ever be enough.

Saint John Paul II, I love you.

CHAPTER ONE
A Still Small Voice

ichael rolled over and groped for the ringing cell phone that was somewhere on his nightstand. With his eyes still shut, he knocked over a glass half full of water. His eyes snapped open and he was thankful to see that the water glass had fallen onto the carpeted floor rather than toppled onto the night stand. Wet rug he could handle, wet cell phone could have been a nightmare.

Snapping open the still ringing phone, he peered over at the clock which read 7:30 a.m. He groaned inwardly — it was Saturday after all.

"Yeah, Michael here," he said, his voice thick with sleep.

For a moment there was no sound at all on the other end and Michael rolled his eyes. Just like his luck to get a stupid sales call or automated robot at seven thirty on a Saturday morning.

"I said, Michael here," he said a little more gruffly.

"Michael?" asked a small voice.

Michael sat up in the bed and scratched his matted hair. "Um-hum."

"Michael, its Kelsey," replied the quavering voice.

"Kelsey, are you okay?" Michael asked. "It's early. It's Saturday."

"I know," said Kelsey. Michael could hear weeping.

He swung his legs over the side of his bed. He was awake for sure now.

"Kelsey, what is it? What's the matter?"

"Are you in Springfield or are you home this weekend?" Kelsey squeaked out. "I need someone to talk to."

Michael got out of bed and started rifling through the pile of clothes on his floor looking for a pair of jeans.

"I'm at my apartment at school, but I can meet you. No problem. Are you at home?"

"Yeah," Kelsey replied. "I got home late last night."

"Do you have a car?" Michael hoped against hope that he wouldn't need to make the one hour drive all the way to Carlstown this morning. He had just gone home last weekend and his bank account was beginning to suffer.

"Yeah, no problem," Kelsey said sniffing loudly. "I can meet you….how about the cappuccino place we always stop at halfway on Route 90.

Cradling the cell phone on his shoulder, Michael tossed the found jeans and a clean shirt onto his bed.

"Yeah, that would work. I really need to shower. If I leave here in twenty minutes I should be able to be there about 9 a.m."

"Thank you, Michael, I'll meet you there." He could almost hear her smiling on the other end of the phone.

"Kels, drive safe," he reminded her.

Michael clicked the phone shut and took a deep breath. This wasn't how he intended to spend his Saturday morning. He glanced at his bed longingly and then scooping up his clothes, stumbled to the shower.

In exactly twenty minutes, Michael was pulling shut the door of his small Ford Focus. He started the car and sat there for a moment praying quietly. Kelsey was a girl from his church youth group. They had been friends throughout high school. He could tell that she was really upset. He hadn't heard from her in the two years that she'd gone on to college and he was curious to know why she would call him now.

Michael grabbed his CD case from the floor of the passenger side and flipped through it looking for a new selection. He pulled out a Third Day CD, ejecting what was already playing. He popped in the new CD, shifted the car into reverse and backed out of the driveway at just before eight-thirty on this bright Saturday morning.

The drive to the cappuccino shop was uneventful. Michael sang along to some of the songs. Traffic remained light, which surprised him for a fall Saturday morning. He pulled off the highway and drove into the parking lot of the small strip mall where the cappuccino shop was located. He didn't know if Kelsey had arrived yet because he didn't know what kind of car she was driving. He figured that he would go in and keep a lookout for her from one of the seats by the window.

As Michael pulled open the door, a din of sound greeted him. People of all sorts were milling about — some waiting in line to be served, some sitting at tables or in the comfy chairs that were set up around the room. Michael did not see Kelsey anywhere, unless she had already arrived and had stepped into the ladies' room. He got in line and looked over the menu, realizing that he had skipped breakfast. When it was his turn, Michael ordered a large hot chocolate and a blueberry muffin.

Looking around for a table or somewhere to sit, Michael waited at the cash register for his order. The muffin was still warm when he picked it up, along with his drink. A two-seater table had just vacated near the window. As Michael was making his way in that direction, he heard someone calling his name. He glanced toward the door and did a double take. Kelsey was standing just inside the door, but she looked nothing like he remembered her. She had jet black hair framing her small face instead of her usual blonde. If she had not called his name, he wouldn't have recognized her.

Putting his stuff onto the table, Michael waved in her direction. She walked hesitantly toward him.

"Hey Kels," he said, leaning over to give her a hug.

"I didn't know if you would recognize me," she confessed, "But you look about the same except your hair is shorter."

"Well, I probably wouldn't have recognized you if I were just walking past you on the street," he laughed. "And speaking of hair, what's with yours?"

Kelsey sank into the chair that would keep her back to the room and Michael took the seat across from her. She didn't respond to his question; she just kept looking at him.

Michael had always been a good-looking guy. His brown hair was cut shorter than Kelsey remembered. He had a well-proportioned face, clean-cut and ruddy from spending time outdoors. He was well built, but not obviously so. His tee-shirt hung about him loosely but Kelsey could still see the outline of his muscles. At five feet one, she felt even smaller beneath his gaze.

"I wasn't sure when you would get here so I got some breakfast," he told her. "Do you want something?"

"Not hungry," she replied quietly.

The vibrant gal with long, wavy blonde hair that he remembered from high school had been replaced by a gaunt, black-haired girl who looked younger than her years and peered at him with scared eyes.

"Mind if I pray?" Michael asked nonchalantly.

Kelsey shook her head, but looked around quickly to

see if anyone was watching them, while Michael intoned the blessing softly.

"You still do that sort of thing?" she asked when Michael began to eat his muffin.

He smiled broadly and nodded. "You don't?"

Kelsey shifted uncomfortably.

Michael pushed his mostly-eaten muffin aside and leaned over the table toward her.

"What's going on, Kelsey?"

She glanced quickly away from his piercing blue eyes.

He wanted to press her for an answer, but he didn't think that she would be receptive to talking about it quite yet.

"How are you enjoying school?" she asked.

"Actually, I love it," he replied, giving her another broad smile. "I still have no idea what I'm going to do with my life, but I'm enjoying it all the same."

Kelsey cracked a smile for the first time since she had arrived.

"Does that mean you are actually doing the coursework?" Michael laughed and after a minute Kelsey joined him. Kelsey had been his saving grace in high school math classes.

"Well," he replied, "I wouldn't go that far."

"It's good to know that some things never change," she told him. "What are you studying?"

"Right now, I'm getting my undergraduate degree in theology. And what are you doing these days?"

"I didn't know that you could get a degree in theology," she remarked.

"It's a Catholic school," he explained.

"Well, I'm still studying nursing. I really love it, but…" Her voice trailed off and Michael saw her hazel eyes well up with tears.

"What's up?" he asked her gently.

11

Michael crumpled up his muffin wrapper and sliding his hot chocolate cup to the side, he put his strong hands over the top of Kelsey's slender ones. He held her small, shaking hands gently in his own and kept silent, just waiting for her to speak.

"I..." Her voice cracked and one tear made its way down her cheek. "I think I might be pregnant."

Michael did not react. He remained perfectly still across the table. When he moved, he stood up so quickly that the crumpled muffin wrapper rolled down off of the tabletop. He pulled Kelsey up into a big hug and she started sobbing into his chest. Michael ignored the stares of the onlookers as he held Kelsey close to him and guided her out of the crowded cappuccino place.

The crisp fall air greeted them full on as they exited the warm cozy atmosphere of the restaurant. Michael led Kelsey, who was still sobbing, around to the passenger side of his car. He opened the door for her and then just stood there holding her until she calmed down a little bit.

"I'm so scared," she whimpered, as she pulled away from him.

He pulled her back into another hug and whispered in her hair.

"It will be okay Kelsey, I'll help you."

She began to cry again.

Michael pushed her gently toward the open door.

"Here, get in and we can talk some more. I think I might have some tissues or napkins in the glove. Do you want me to go inside and get some more?"

Kelsey shook her head and sank into the seat. She pulled out a large wad of Kleenex that had been stashed in the pocket of her oversized hoodie.

Michael shut the door firmly and rounded the car to get in the other side. As he did so, he looked around for a more secluded parking spot where they wouldn't be seen by every person walking up and down the sidewalks of the strip mall.

"Let's pull over there," Michael pointed, starting up the car. "So we can talk with a little more privacy."

"I guess the cappuccino place wasn't such a great idea," Kelsey sniffed. "I thought if I were in a room full of people that I wouldn't go to pieces like that." Her dark hair hung loose, framing her small face.

Michael guided the car back a few rows and over to the side where they would be out of the fray of most of the traffic. He put the car in park but left the heater on.

"Do you want to talk about it?" Michael asked after a minute. He looked over at Kelsey who had stopped crying.

"I don't know what I'm going to do," she replied.

"How did this happen?"

Kelsey looked over at him and laughed viciously. Michael laughed, too.

"That's not what I meant," he told her, "I know how it happened! I'm just wondering why or ..." His voice trailed off.

"I know," Kelsey said bitterly. "How could I do such a thing?!"

"That's not what I said," Michael told her quietly.

"It's so stupid," she whispered.

"I'm not judging you Kelsey," he assured her. "If this is the reality, then we need to face it and figure out what to do from here."

"There's nothing to figure out," Kelsey told him. "I know what I'm going to do."

Michael searched her face, but she turned away. He watched the back of her head as she gazed out the window and prayed silently to St. Michael the Archangel.

The two of them did not speak as the car continued running and the slightest hint of Third Day drifted through the speakers.

"I don't need a lecture," Kelsey spat, after a moment, twisting quickly to look at him.

"Then why did you call me?" Michael asked her.

Kelsey sat sullenly in the passenger seat. She closed her eyes, trying to block out the world.

"I remember when my life was so simple," she whispered, "before any of this."

She lifted up a handful of her black hair.

"I'm not sure what happened, or when it happened. When I got to Chatham University, I had a hard time fitting in. Everyone there parties all the time. I tried to pray when I first got there."

She opened her eyes and fixed them on Michael.

"Really, I did try to pray."

He nodded.

"It just got to be so hard. And God wasn't listening to me anyway. So I met some people in my Chem class. They were all the hard science types. We would talk for hours about God, the creation of the Universe. They gave me a book to read, The God Delusion. I thought it was really good and I wanted to be free of all those rules… Then I started hanging out with Adam."

"Is Adam the father?" Michael asked.

"I swear to you Michael, it was only one time! I don't know what happened. I didn't plan it – I never intended for things to get so out of control."

Kelsey started to cry quietly again.

"Does Adam know?"

Kelsey shook her head.

"You need to tell him."

"Why? What difference does it make if he knows?"

"How long have you two been together?" he asked.

"About six months."

"And how pregnant are you?" he asked.

"This is the second month I missed."

"Are you two still sleeping together?"

Kelsey looked at Michael defiantly.

"I told you it was only one time."

"Well, that just seems weird to me, Kels," Michael told her. "What did you tell him after the first time, that you weren't going to sleep with him again and he just let you off the hook?"

"That's a mean thing to say!" Kelsey shot. "We agreed it was a mistake!"

Michael nodded.

"If that's really true, then he sounds like he could be a decent guy. He has a right to know. It's his baby too."

Kelsey remained sullenly silent.

"Why did you call me?" Michael finally asked her again.

"Because I can trust you; I knew that you would help me," she replied.

Michael leveled a long hard look at Kelsey.

"I will help you in any way that I can," he told her gently, "but I will not help you to get an abortion."

Kelsey burst into tears again, and looked away.

"I'm so scared Michael; what am I going to do?" she whispered.

Michael reached over and put his strong hand on her slender shoulder.

"Look at me, Kels."

She slowly turned to look back at him with haunted hazel eyes.

"Did you take a pregnancy test? Are you absolutely sure that you're pregnant?"

She shook her head no.

"Okay, this is what we're going to do then," he commanded.

"I'm going in there to get you a muffin for breakfast and then you are going to follow me back to Springfield."

Michael could see his day of working on his research paper for PoliSci quickly drifting away.

"Then we're going to get you a pregnancy test and only after we get the results will we talk any more about what you are going to do....Deal?"

Kelsey took a deep breath and nodded her head. Michael let go of her shoulder after giving her a quick, friendly shake. He turned off the car, got out and walked Kelsey back over to her car. He went back into the cappuccino place to order another blueberry muffin. He brought the muffin, along with an orange juice, over to Kelsey who was sitting in her quietly idling Honda Civic.

"I live at Rookwood Manor Apartments," Michael told her while handing the food in through the window. "You can follow me, but if you have a GPS, you might want to plug it in."

Kelsey leaned over to open her glove and pulled out a portable GPS.

"You shouldn't leave that in there, you know," Michael told her. "If anyone sees you putting it in there, they'll break into your car to take it."

"You sound like my father," Kelsey chided him. She asked him to repeat the address as she entered it into the GPS. Michael shook his head and walked back to his own car.

Once back inside, he bowed his head and blew out a big breath. The day was going to be a stressful one; there was no way around that.

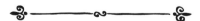

The ride back to Springfield was as equally uneventful as the drive out. Just the same, Michael kept checking the rear view mirror to make sure Kelsey hadn't turned around.

When they arrived, Kelsey pulled her car into a parking space right alongside of Michael next to what she guessed was the building where his apartment was located. He didn't get out of the car, but instead rolled down his window and called to her, "Get in."

Kelsey closed her car door and running around, got back into the passenger side of Michael's car.

"I thought it would be easier to take one car to the pharmacy," he explained as she clicked on her seat belt. "It's right around the corner."

They drove the few minutes in silence. Kelsey looked like she was surveying the gallows as Michael drove her into a parking place right next to the entrance.

"Buy two," he said.

Kelsey pushed open the car door and walked dejectedly into the store. Michael stayed in the car. He pulled out his cell phone and punching two buttons, listened to the ringing on the other end.

"Hello, Michael" said a soft female voice.

"Anna, hey – how are you?" he asked smiling.

"I'm fine and you?"

"Well, it's going to be a long day I think. I've got a friend who seems to be in some trouble. Are you going to be home later on? I think she might need a woman to talk to…"

"I've got to work in a couple of hours, but I get out at 6:00," Anna replied.

"How about your parents? Are they going to be home tonight?" he asked.

"Yeah, I think everyone will be here. There's a chance that Hope will be coming by later on for a movie - with her daughters. She may or may not bring Jessica and Stephen with her."

Michael knit his brow. He did not want Kelsey to be

overwhelmed by people, but he knew these were the folks that could make a difference to her now.

Michael looked up and through the large glass window. He could see Kelsey at the cash register.

"I've got to go, but would you please pray for my friend, and ask your family too?" he asked hurriedly.

"Sure Michael, maybe I'll see you later," Anna responded.

"I'll call first to let you guys know."

"That would be great," she said. "Have a good day."

Michael cringed inwardly, "Yeah, you too." He flipped the phone shut just as Kelsey was walking out of the store clutching a small bag to her chest. She looked positively green.

"You okay?" Michael asked as she slid into the seat next to him.

She lowered her head, her dark hair creating a curtain which hid her face.

"Is there something wrong? Did something happen?" he asked, turning around to back out of the parking spot.

"The cashier gave me a business card," Kelsey said quietly. "She realized that I was purchasing two pregnancy tests and so she said she was putting a business card into the bag. If I needed any help I could call the number on the card."

Michael sat seething as he drove slowly out of the parking lot and onto the street.

"Did you see it?" he asked.

Kelsey shook her head.

"Give it to me," he demanded.

She quickly pulled out a small, pink business card and placed it into Michael's open palm. He glanced at it quickly. It said only *Chelsea's Choice* and had a toll-free number printed beneath the words. Michael crumpled up the card in his hand.

"That's just the kind of help you don't need," he told Kelsey, who had begun to cry again silently.

18

Driving back to the apartment, Michael pulled his car into the parking spot next to Kelsey's small blue Honda. He shut off the car and did a quick scan of the area.

"My roommates are out," he announced, getting out of the car and walking around to open Kelsey's door. She stuffed a used Kleenex back into the pocket of her hoodie and took Michael's offered hand.

Taking her hand gently, Michael helped her out of the car. Putting an arm around her waist, he led her over to the entrance door and up the steps as she continued to sniffle. His place was on the second floor. After letting them into the small two bedroom apartment, Michael directed Kelsey to the couch. She sat down heavily and he left to go to the kitchen to make some tea.

"I put water on for tea or instant coffee," he told her, coming to sit beside her on the sofa. "Or I have water, if you would rather."

"I'll wait for tea," Kelsey replied.

"Let's read the directions," he suggested.

"This is so stupid Michael!" Kelsey exclaimed, jumping up from the sofa. "What options do I really have anyway?"

She started to pace back and forth before the fireplace, rubbing her hands up and down her arms as if she were cold.

"I've already told you," Michael reminded her gently. "We don't need to even think about any of that before you take the test."

She stopped pacing and turned to look at him, dropping her hands to her sides.

"I know you're scared," he told her. "Let's just get this test over with and see what happens. I've got two sisters; I know that sometimes women skip months and it's no big deal."

"But I've never missed a month before…never…ever!"

Michael just nodded his head. "Okay, but let's not freak

out until we get the results of the test."

Kelsey watched as he tore open one of packages of the home pregnancy tests. He scanned the directions quickly.

"Seems easy," he murmured.

She continued to stand, watching him silently.

"Are you ready to do this?" he asked.

Her eyes filled with tears.

"Do you want to pray?"

"Don't be stupid," Kelsey barked, "What good will that do?!" She strode over and ripped the package out of his hand.

"You didn't used to think it was so stupid," he told her gently, placing his hand on her shoulder and trying to look into her eyes.

"Where's your bathroom?" She twisted away from his grasp and lowering her eyes, she walked down the hall.

"First door on the left."

The tea kettle whistled and Michael got up to make two cups of tea. Kelsey slammed the bathroom door loudly. He bustled nervously around the kitchen looking for sugar. He always took his tea with cream only, but he wanted to have sugar to offer Kelsey.

A few minutes went by and still she didn't come out. Michael glanced at the clock — 11:43. He was wondering how long he should leave her alone in there when the bathroom door clicked open and Kelsey came around into the kitchen. She looked pale as a sheet.

"My hands were shaking so badly that it was kinda hard to do," she told him, looking down.

Michael rubbed his hand along her arm and went to hand her the cup of tea. When he saw that her hands were still shaking badly, he set the tea on the counter and took her hands gently into his own.

"Kelsey, I promise you this will all work out somehow,"

he told her.

She did not respond.

He squeezed her hands tightly and let them go. She raised her scared eyes to look at him.

Glancing at the clock he asked, "Do you want me to go and check it?"

She nodded.

He led her back to the sofa, brought her tea from the kitchen and then went quietly into the bathroom down the hall. As Michael stepped into the room, he said another quick Hail Mary and walked slowly over to the toilet where the pregnancy test was sitting on the white ceramic back. If the red "+" sign had been made of blinking neon lights it would have seemed dimmer than the bold red mark looking up at him from the white tester packet.

Michael didn't realize that he was gripping the side of the counter so forcefully until he heard Kelsey's small voice call him from the living room.

"Michael?"

He scooped up the white plastic test holder and carried it in the paper it was sitting on back into the living room and stood facing Kelsey.

"Positive?" she asked, almost choking.

"It'll be alright Kels," he assured her as she buried her face in her hands and started to sob again. "Let me toss this out."

When Michael came back from the kitchen, Kelsey had curled herself up into a ball on the living room sofa and had her eyes squeezed shut.

"My life is so over," she whispered as the tears continued to run down her cheeks.

Michael knelt on the floor next to her and taking her hand in his, he just held it, feeling completely sick to his stomach.

There had to be some way that he could talk some sense into Kelsey to make sure that she did right by this new baby.

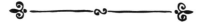

Kelsey had fallen asleep on the sofa at about twelve-thirty so Michael took advantage of the quiet to see if he could get any work done on his paper for PoliSci. He sat at his computer in the smaller of the two bedrooms and stared at the screen for what seemed like ages. He should have known he would never be able to concentrate with the weight of Kelsey's discovery sitting like an anvil in the pit of his stomach. He rearranged some words in this paragraph and reworked some ideas in that one. He never made any headway with the writing process, but at least he could tell himself that he had tried.

At three o'clock, Michael checked his email — nothing important there, just a note from his brother James, who was at Quinnipiac in Connecticut. The two guys had been trying to plan a time to meet somewhere in the middle since James had left for his first semester. Now, because of Michael's dwindling financial situation and the new circumstances with Kelsey, Michael didn't think they would be meeting up any time soon. He said as much in his reply email, leaving off the details about Kelsey's personal situation. James and Kelsey knew each other, though not well, and Michael did not want to go about spreading her personal business around.

After sending out the email, Michael headed out into the living room to wake Kelsey from her nap. She was already sitting up on the sofa when he came down the hall.

"Did you sleep okay?" he asked her, sliding onto the sofa next to her.

She nodded. "I'm sorry," she said hollowly.

"For what?" he asked.

"For dragging you into the middle of my mess," she told

him.

Michael smiled. "Well, that's what friends are for," he reminded her, "Also, I don't see any baby as a mess."

Kelsey looked at him intently.

"I know this isn't how you planned things, Kels. I know that many women don't plan these things, but I do know that abortion is never the answer."

"How can it not be?" she asked in a strangled voice.

Michael took her hand. "Look, there are some people that I'd like you to meet…"

Kelsey shook her head vigorously.

"They are good friends of mine, Kels, and they will be good friends to you to," he explained.

"I don't know," she began. "Look at me, I'm a mess."

"Do you trust me?" he asked her.

"Yeah…that's why I called you," she replied.

"Well first, you need to call Adam and tell him what's going on. Then you need to come with me tonight over to my friend's house. There's going to be a couple of women that I know – they are both single moms."

Kelsey bristled visibly.

"Not for that reason," Michael said, "but because they are both friends of mine with experience with babies and because they can help you to face what you are going through. Do you have a doctor?"

"Are you kidding?" Kelsey asked.

"No Kels, I'm completely serious. Regardless of what happens next, you are pregnant and you and the baby need to get checked out by a good doctor," he said.

Kelsey leaned back into the sofa, putting some distance between her and Michael. "Michael, there's no way…"

Michael held up his hand. "Listen," he said. "You owe it to yourself, to Adam and to this new baby not to make any rash decisions. I know you don't want a baby. I know that you don't feel ready for a baby and I'm sure you think that Adam feels the same way. Truth is - he probably does. But you know what Kels, there are tons of people who are just sitting around dying to adopt a little baby girl or boy."

Kelsey's eyes began to fill with tears again. "I don't know..."

"Look, you just found out what's going on," he reminded her, "Give yourself a break. You're overwhelmed. You're freaked out. You feel completely alone."

"How do you know all that?" Kelsey asked.

Michael gave her a long look and took a deep breath.

"Because," Michael replied after a moment, "my sister had a baby and gave him up for adoption."

Kelsey looked at Michael with wide eyes.

"I know an awful lot about what you are thinking and feeling," he told her.

Just then the door of the apartment burst open and Michael's two roommates — Dave and Justin — both bounded loudly into the room.

They were talking and laughing at once when they noticed Michael and Kelsey sitting on the sofa across from them. Michael stood up.

"I didn't know you were going to be hanging out here with someone," Justin said suspiciously.

"Hi," Dave said.

"Guys, this is my friend Kelsey. She's from my old church youth group," Michael explained. "She came up here so we could talk. She's in a bit of a tough spot and I'm going to help her out."

"Hello," Kelsey said quietly, averting her eyes.

Justin got out of his jacket while looking her over. He shook his head imperceptibly and Michael shot him an angry look.

Dave, on the other hand, walked directly into the kitchen.

"Are you two going to be staying here for supper?" he called pleasantly.

"No, we're getting together with some friends," Michael replied.

"Is everything okay?" Justin directed his question to Michael who was helping Kelsey to get up.

"Not really, no," Michael replied honestly, "but it will be. We've got a lot of people that we can turn to… everything will be okay." He was talking to both Justin and Kelsey.

Michael led Kelsey over to pick up her jacket. He helped her into it. Kelsey walked out the door first.

"Is she your girlfriend?" Justin asked, moving quickly to catch hold of the door before Michael did.

"No, Justin," Michael replied, sliding out past him. "I told you, she's just a friend of mine from my old youth group and she needs a little help right now, it's fine."

CHAPTER TWO
Closing the Circle

As they walked down the steps of the apartment complex, Michael called Anna Warner's house. The Warners had four children and were a strong, Catholic family. Pizza was on the menu for the evening since there was uncertainty about the numbers that would arrive in time to eat, so Anna said, "You and your friend —what's her name by the way? — can pitch in for the pizza after you get here."

"Her name is Kelsey. And thank your mother for us."

Kelsey followed Michael in her own car because she didn't want to feel trapped once she got there.

The drive to Hadley did not take long; traffic was still light. The trees had all changed colors and most of the leaves had already fallen off. Michael turned into the parking lot of the local grocery store with Kelsey still close behind him. They parked side-by-side in a couple of empty spaces. Michael motioned for Kelsey to roll down her window.

"I'm just going to run in and grab a couple of bottles of soda," he explained, "...any preference?"

"I like Diet Coke," she replied.

Michael frowned. "That stuff is trash."

She gave a long-suffering sigh and fixed him with her hazel eyes. "Ginger Ale?"

"Better." He smiled at her and then was trotting down the aisle toward the store. Kelsey rolled up her window and leaned her head back against the seat, clicking the heater up a notch and peering over at her cell phone that was charging while on the ride. She felt completely empty and despairing.

You need to call Adam. She could hear Michael's husky voice clear as a bell in her head.

Kelsey reached over and picked up the phone. She hit the number for quick dial but did not hit the send key. She looked at the little picture of her and Adam that popped up when she chose his contact info. The two of them were goofing around. His brother had taken the picture of them making funny faces. She suddenly felt sick....what would she say? How would he react?

She tossed the phone back onto her passenger seat and clicked on the radio instead. Classic Metallica came blaring through her speakers. She immediately felt that same tightening in her stomach and clicked it off almost immediately. When had she started listening to Metallica? Leaning her head back onto the seat, Kelsey blew out a big breath. She looked at her dim reflection in the rearview mirror. She studied her face, drawn with the stress of the situation, her hazel eyes staring dully back at her., the black hair hanging severely past her chin. She did not even know who she was any more. How could she know what to do about this situation?

Her cell phone chirruped. Great, now she would need to deal with her mother.

"Hey Mom," Kelsey said trying to sound normal.

"Hi Kelsey. " Her mother's voice was grating to her ears. "Where are you? Will you be home for dinner?"

Kelsey cringed. She knew how much her mom hated

it when she missed dinner on the rare weekends that she was back from college. "Um, no Mom, I'm not going to make it tonight," she said.

"Oh," her mother replied noncommittally. "Watcha doin?"

Figuring out what to do about being pregnant, Kelsey thought to herself. Aloud she said, "Actually Mom, I'm hanging out with my friend, Michael. I'm sure you remember him... you know...."

"You mean Michael Anderson?" her mother asked, interrupting quickly.

"Yeah, that's the one," Kelsey replied, rolling her eyes, "from my old church youth group."

"Oh, that's lovely honey. I didn't know you two stayed in touch." Her mother's voice was all charm.

"We just reconnected recently," Kelsey told her. She did not say that by recently she actually meant just this morning.

"He's a wonderful boy," her mother gushed.

"I'm glad you like him, Mom."

"Is Adam with you?" Her mother tried to sound disinterested as she asked the question.

"No, why?" Kelsey asked. She rolled her eyes again.

"Oh, I was just wondering." Her mother's voice trailed off in a peal of nervous laughter.

"I gotta go, Mom," Kelsey said.

"Sure, sure, dear." said her mother, talking over her. "Be careful driving home."

"See you later. Bye, Mom."

"Bye Kels."

Kelsey clicked the phone shut and immediately it rang again. This time it was Adam. Kelsey peered at the little photo of the two of them clowning around and then the sight of Michael loading his car caught her eye so she looked up.

Hurriedly, she sent the call to voice mail. Adam would be mad. He hated it when she did not take his calls. She sighed loudly. There would be much more for him to hate about her once she got up the guts to tell him about the situation.

Michael waved to Kelsey as he sat down in his driver's seat. She waved back indicating that she was ready to go. The Warner house was just a few minutes further down the road. As Kelsey followed Michael's lead and parked on the rural neighborhood street, all the wind seemed knocked out of her. She struggled to breath; her temper flared. What was Michael thinking? She had no intention of going inside to meet a group of total strangers that would look at her like she was a charity case.

Michael opened her door with one hand and held the paper bags of soda with the other.

"How do I get to the highway?" she asked through clenched teeth. "I talked to my mom before and she's expecting me home for dinner."

"Oh," Michael replied, giving her a long look.

Kelsey knew that he didn't believe her.

"Well, if you let me drop these bottles off inside, I'll lead you back," he said pleasantly, letting this one go.

Kelsey fidgeted.

"In fact, why don't you take one of these bags and help a man out?" Michael suggested smiling.

Kelsey scowled. "I'm not going in there."

"They are really great people Kelsey," he told her softly.

She nodded. "I'm sure they are," she relented, "but I'm still not going in there."

"Alright, give me a sec," he said, closing her door again. She watched him quickly cross the street and knock on the wooden front door.

In a moment, the door was opened by a cute little girl

about the age of five. She had straight brown hair pulled up in a ponytail with a white ribbon bow clipped to it. She hopped around excitedly clapping her hands, a wide smile on her pretty face. Kelsey watched Michael and the little girl talking animatedly. In another moment, a lanky yet athletic teen boy in a gray muscle shirt and ball cap and a dark haired older gentleman in jeans and a polo shirt, who probably was the father of the family, appeared on the other side of the door. The boy took the bags from Michael and the man shook his hand heartily. Kelsey could see Michael gesture in her direction. She wanted to sink down into the seat. The three people hanging out of the doorway waved at her as she turned her head away. She didn't want to be rude, so she gestured a small wave but continued looking away. She started a moment later when there was a tap on her car window.

Rolling the window down just a crack, she heard Michael say "Ok then, follow me to the highway. I'll get you back onto Route 3 and you can get yourself back from there."

Kelsey nodded and shifted the car into drive impatiently. She glanced at the door of the house which was shut now and felt a pang of sadness. They looked like nice people and under other circumstances she was sure she would have liked them. She shook her head quickly and followed Michael back out the windy roads of the small neighborhood and back past the same grocery store. After about five minutes, Kelsey saw the big green Interstate sign on her left. Michael pulled into the commuter lot just before the entrance ramp and Kelsey waved to him as she drove on by.

She merged onto the highway seconds later and then her phone rang once more. This time it was Michael. She clicked on her ear piece.

"Hey," he said even before she greeted him. "You just stay cool and don't do anything crazy without talking to me first, ok? And you really need to tell Adam."

"Yeah, yeah, okay," Kelsey responded. "Have a fun dinner with your friends."

"I'm sorry you decided not to come," Michael told her.

She paused as she noted the real sincerity in his voice.

"I've gotta get back," she stammered.

"Yeah, that's cool. I remember your mom is a good cook," Michael said. "You can have pizza any ol' time at school; I understand."

Kelsey laughed. She really did like this handsome, brown-haired, tall, warm-hearted guy, even if her life was going all to pieces right now. He was a good friend and she was thankful.

"My mom says Hi by the way," Kelsey told him, remembering her mother's new found excitement that Kelsey would be seeing Michael.

"Hi back."

"Okay, I'll talk to you soon then," Kelsey said.

"Sounds good," Michael agreed.

"And Michael…thank you."

"Take it easy, Kelsey. I promise everything will be alright."

Back at the Warner house, Michael rang the bell and waited on the steps for someone to open the door. His whole weekend was down the drain at this point anyway, so he figured he might as well come back for some pizza, fellowship and perhaps some ideas on what to do about Kelsey.

This time, it was the father who opened the door. Timothy Warner embraced Michael in a big one armed hug which contrasted deeply with his imposing and serious figure.

"Hey man, glad you came back."

"Yeah, me too," Michael told him.

"Michael!" Lucy was squealing his name. He bent down

and scooped the little pony-tailed cutie up in a big hug as well.

"We never see you anymore," she protested.

"Lucy!" Timothy admonished.

"Well, I'm here now," Michael reminded her.

"Yay! Are you staying for dinner?" Lucy asked, as he placed her over the stoop and back onto the floor.

Michael was nodding his head as Lucy's brother Zack came around the corner and gave him a hearty handshake as he stepped in from outdoors. As usual, Zack's handshake was more like a wrestling grip than a sincerely friendly gesture and Zack grinned wickedly.

"Everyone's in the kitchen."

Michael followed Zack down the short hallway, darting quickly to knock the ball cap Zack always wore from his head.

"No hats in the house," Michael reminded him teasingly.

Zack grinned sheepishly, tucking the cap beneath his arm, as they both walked into the kitchen where Lily, Timothy's wife; Anna, Michael's friend; and her younger sister, Jane, were getting paper goods out of the pantry.

"Hey everyone," Michael said.

Lily stepped back out of the pantry, rubbing her hands on her black jeans.

"I recognize that long-lost voice!"

"Hey Michael," Anna said. "It's good to see you."

Michael looked for a time at his friend but had to turn away as he felt the blush rise on the back of his neck. He had always thought that Anna was attractive, with her wavy dark hair, deep brown eyes and fabulous figure. She had filled out even more since the last time he had seen her. She looked more like a woman now in her knee-length blue dress with light blue leggings and white shrug. She was no longer the little girl he once knew.

Lily came over and gave Michael a quick squeeze,

distracting him from his thoughts.

"You look a bit thinner," she remarked, standing back to give him the once over.

"Bachelor living," he told her, smiling ruefully and rubbing the back of his neck. He hoped that she wouldn't comment on his flaming complexion. Lily met his eyes and smiled kindly. She knew her daughter was beautiful inside and out and she was pleased that a nice guy like Michael would notice that too.

"Everyone else is coming too, with all their kids." Lucy announced happily, allowing Michael to breath a sigh of relief that the awkward moment had passed.

"That's great!" Michael exclaimed. "I can see everyone at once." He knew by "everyone else," Lucy meant his friends, Jessica and Hope, the single moms who he was so anxious for Kelsey to meet.

To Lucy, Michael said, "When are the others coming?"

"Mom, when are the others coming?" Lucy asked, looking over her shoulder at her mother who was slender with curly dark hair.

"Everyone should be here by six," Lily replied, the laugh lines in her face reflecting the gratitude she felt to have such great friends and family. "I'm sorry that your friend, Kelsey – is that her name? – couldn't join us." A shadow passed over Lily's face.

Michael nodded knowingly. "Yeah, me too."

"Hey man, Zack and I are downstairs trying to hook up this old turntable to this old laptop if you're interested," Timothy explained, opening the door to the basement. Zack darted past him and headed down the stairs.

"Cool, I'm right behind you. I just need a minute up here," Michael responded to the retreating footsteps.

"Michael, can I get you something to drink?" Lily asked,

coming around from behind the kitchen island and wiping her fair hands on a checkered dishtowel.

"Water would be great," he replied.

"Jane, get Michael some water, please," Lily instructed.

"Mrs. Warner, if you don't need Anna at the moment, I'd like to talk to her about helping my friend Kelsey," Michael said.

Lily looked up at him with concern. She thought for a moment, hesitated, and then replied, "Sure, why don't you go out to the back deck where little ears won't hear you?"

Jane handed Michael his water and made to follow them out onto the deck.

"No Jane," Lily said, "I need you to watch Lucy."

"But Mom," Jane began, tugging on her braid and getting ready to argue.

Michael gave Jane a placating look and pulled the door shut. He could see Jane, hands on her hips, talking heatedly to her mother who was still shaking her head no.

When they had seated themselves on the glider rocker, Michael got right to the heart of the matter: "Well, it seems that this girl I know from my old church group is pregnant."

"Oh, wow," Anna said softly, she pushed a lock of dark hair behind her ear.

He nodded.

"Has she said what she's going to do about it?" Anna was almost afraid to ask.

"I don't think she's made any decision yet," he told her. "I let her know that I have a bunch of resources and people who can help her."

Anna nodded. "Was she too scared to come in to see us?"

"Yeah, she decided to go home."

She nodded again.

"I would have liked to talk to her." Anna's eyes grew sad with compassion and she fingered the small earring hanging from her ear.

"So how far along are we talking?" she asked, gently rocking them both on the glider and clasping her hands in her lap.

"No more than two months from what she's told me."

Loud banter from the kitchen disrupted their conversation. Hope, a middle aged woman, slim in black corduroy pants with a hand knit red sweater had arrived, bringing her two teen daughters, Alicia and Rachel. Both teen girls were already taller than their mother as they stood together greeting the Warners. Alicia looked comfortable in her jeans and Third Day hoodie and her younger sister, Rachel, looked fashionable in her brown knit sweater dress and matching leggings. Jessica, a shorter young woman with strawberry blond hair and her 10 year old son, Stephen, were also with them. Stephen has Cerebral Palsy and looks as if he's about 7. He works harder than most to walk and communicate, but his frequent smiles light up the whole room.

Michael, carrying Lucy, had come in to greet everyone and jumped into the middle of the kitchen yelling like a crazy person which made Stevie jump; Anna followed, a sad smile tugging on the corners of her lips. Everyone laughed at Stevie's response and then talked at the same time. Michael took turns hugging Jessica, Hope and the rest of the gang.

"I haven't seen you guys in forever," he said to the room in general.

"We can't help it if you're such a stranger," Jessica replied stripping off her sweatshirt and wearing just her bright orange tee-shirt and jeans. "It's warm in here."

"You sound just like my mother."

Everyone laughed.

"Then you shouldn't be homesick."

The room bustled with activity. Lily set the pizzas onto the counter; Jane was pouring drinks; Hope pulled out forks, and Jessica had turned to cut up a piece of pizza for her disabled son. Stephen, whom she had taught to do many things, still couldn't handle a knife on his own.

"Tim," Lily called, "dinner!"

Lucy sauntered to the basement door and, yanking it open, yelled down, "Dad! Dinner!"

The guys bounded up the steps and as Timothy walked into the center of the kitchen everything went silent.

"Let's pray," he said. Everyone gathered in a small circle, bowed their heads and intoned together, "Bless us O Lord, and these thy gifts which we are about to receive from thy bounty through Christ our Lord. Amen."

"Do the kids go first?" Jane asked when they had finished, helping herself to a paper plate. She tossed her braid and pushed her glasses quickly up on her nose.

"Jane, we have guests," Lily reminded her daughter as she motioned for the other kids to help themselves.

"But Zack will eat it all!" Jane protested.

"You need to wait," Lily whispered. "Zack will have to wait too."

Jane pouted and moved to the back of the line, yanking on her brother's shirt as she did so.

"Hey!" Zack exclaimed.

"Mom said wait," Jane told him.

"I'm waiting; I'm waiting!"

Once more, the room broke into the happy sounds of laughter and conversation. Two tables were set up to accommodate all of the visitors. The teens and younger kids would be eating in the kitchen. The adults went off into the dining room. Jessica was getting Stephen set up between

Hope's girls, Alicia, 16 and Rachel, 13. Since the two single moms lived next door to one another, the girls were used to helping Stephen out.

"Are you sure that you don't want Stephen to eat in here with me?" Jessica asked again.

Rachel swatted Jessica on the arm as she slid into her seat next to Stephen. She and Stephen were both so thin that they were sitting in the chairs against the wall side.

"You're just jealous because you know he'd rather sit with us," Rachel told her, twisting her long brown hair up into a knot at the back of her neck.

"Is that true Stephen? Would you rather sit with the kids?" Jessica asked, turning to her son.

Stephen smiled broadly and raised his hand for yes.

"See, he didn't even have to think that time," Alicia said coming over to the table.

Jessica handed Alicia the fork, bit her playfully on the arm and then went back to the line to get her own dinner while she and Alicia laughed in unison.

"Michael, you and Anna join us in here," Timothy instructed as he left the kitchen with his plate.

Michael slid into the seat between Timothy who was broad and tall and Jessica who was full-figured and much shorter; Anna sat opposite him with Hope, who even at forty often passed for an older sister when with her daughters.

"What happened to your friend?" Timothy asked in his deep baritone.

"You mean tonight or in general?"

"Both," Timothy replied.

"Well, she decided to head back to Carlstown," Michael explained.

"Is everything okay?" Hope interrupted, tugging her red sweater tighter around her shoulders.

"She was a bit overwhelmed by the prospect of meeting you all. We need to pray for her," Michael finished, raking his fingers through his short hair.

"Michael said she's pregnant," Anna stated quietly, looking at her father.

The room suddenly became silent.

"Yeah," Michael said after a moment, "She came up to tell me this morning. She's freaking out and she doesn't know what to do. I think she needed a friend."

"How long have you known her?" Anna asked, turning her attention back to Michael.

"Since high school."

"Does the baby's father know?" Lily asked, twisting a lock of her curly hair around her finger, a small frown pulling down the sides of her lips.

No one was eating their pizza.

"I hope by now he does," Michael told her. "I said it was a non-negotiable." Heads around the table nodded in agreement.

"Does she have a plan?" Jessica asked Michael, almost regretfully.

The intake of breath around the table happened all at once.

"Thankfully not yet," he said, "or at least, she didn't when she left here."

Everyone seemed to breathe again at the same time.

"Is she open to having the baby?" Timothy asked the question on everyone's mind.

"I'm hoping for that, too," Michael answered. "I had hoped that Anna would be able to meet her and that they could talk."

"Well, I can understand her not wanting to meet a house full of strangers." Jessica tossed her strawberry blonde hair as she gazed at him levelly. "Was tonight really the best night?"

she demanded.

"I didn't really have a plan," Michael said, his voice beginning to escalate.

Timothy held up a hand in warning. The tension in the room had just increased dramatically. Everyone knew, without saying, just exactly what was at stake.

"I think we should offer a Rosary for her after dinner," Lily proposed her tone soft and sensible.

"The kids could join in too," Hope suggested.

"She did the right thing to call you," Jessica reassured Michael, putting her hand on his forearm.

"What if I didn't do enough?" he asked, meeting her gaze and voicing the concern that had been weighing on him all day.

"What more could you do?" Timothy asked.

Lily said quickly, "You were there, you listened, you supported her and I'm guessing that you told her abortion was not the right option?"

"I tried." Michael lowered his head and sighed heavily.

Jessica patted Michael's arm reassuringly.

"You're a good friend," Anna said in her quiet voice. "I'm sure you did exactly the right thing."

Michael met her large brown eyes. "Thank you."

After a moment more of heavy silence, he asked, "Can we talk about something else for a while?"

"How are things going for Stephen at the new school?" Lily asked, artfully changing the subject.

"How are things at Our Lady of Guadalupe?" Hope asked Michael at the same time.

"How was work?" Timothy asked Anna over-top of everyone else.

Those around the table laughed and then so did the kids in the other room.

"What's funny in there?" Timothy called.

"Just Stephen being silly," Jane responded.

"He's so silly," Lucy called; then all the kids laughed again.

"And he knows it," Zack added.

After dinner was finished, the girls cleaned up the tables while Zack wrestled playfully with Stephen on the family room floor.

"You're so mean Zack," Rachel accused, walking into the family room. "You never let Stevie push you over."

"M-M-Mean?" Zack stuttered. "I'm no push over!" He started laughing. "Get it?" he asked, "No push over."

"You're a dork," Alicia told him, dropping onto the sofa.

He made a face at her and Stephen started laughing a good belly laugh. Immediately, everyone was laughing with him.

The adults had moved into the living room and were talking quietly. Michael stuck his head around the corner and called toward the kitchen.

"When you are finished in there your folks want to say a Rosary."

"Did you hear that Stevie?" Zack asked, raising himself up and off of Stephen's pinned shoulder. "We're going to say a Rosary."

Stevie struggled to sit up and then held up his hand high.

"Can I help you up?" Lucy offered.

Zack gently guided Lucy as she helped Stevie to his feet, just as Jane stuffed the last paper plate into the trash.

"I'm ready," Jane told them, "Let's go."

"More chairs please, Zack," Timothy asked as the kids began filing into the living room.

Zack deposited Stevie onto the sofa next to Jessica and went back around to the dining room with Michael to get a few chairs.

"Who are we praying for?" Lucy asked, squeezing up

next to Stephen.

"We'll all take turns," her father promised.

Once the seats were filled and the remaining kids sat on the floor, Timothy began the Rosary with the sign of the cross.

"We'll start with Lucy and you can each offer an intention," he told them.

"I would like to pray for Mrs. Vance, my piano teacher," Lucy said solemnly.

Each person in the circle then stated their intention: improvement of the economy, good grades in school, for Kelsey to make the right decision, for an end to abortion and for Stevie. Just as Timothy was going to start the first prayer, Lucy interrupted with a puzzled look on her face.

"Who's Kelsey?" she asked curiously.

"Kelsey is a friend of mine," Michael told her. "God has asked her to do something very difficult for her and so we are all going to pray for her."

Lucy nodded solemnly and Timothy began the first prayer in his deep baritone. Those sitting in the circle took turns leading the prayers. Even little Lucy led on her own.

At the end of the rosary, it was just about nine o'clock. Both Stephen and Lucy had fallen asleep, heads rested together, sitting in the corner of the sofa.

"What dolls!" Jessica said quietly. "Lily do you have your camera?"

"Jane, could you get the camera?" Lily asked turning to her middle daughter who was already standing. "It's next to the computer."

The older kids, Anna, Rachel, and Alicia, quietly put the chairs back and went back into the family room to talk. Jane brought Lily the camera and went out to be with the other girls.

"Mom, can I get on the computer?" Zack asked.

"No."

"Oh, come on! I want to show Alicia the new game I found on Facebook."

"No Zack. Maybe later," his father responded.

Zack shuffled dejectedly out of the room.

"So, how is your new priest?" Michael asked. "Anna mentioned that Fr. Jeff had been reassigned."

Lily and Timothy shared a long look.

"What's going on?" Hope asked, noticing the look that had passed between her friends.

"Well, it seems our new pastor has some independent ideas," Timothy allowed, trying to find a charitable way to respond.

Jessica frowned. "What does that mean?"

"He performed a wedding just last week where the bride was not Catholic and yet, he invited her and her whole family to receive the Eucharist," Lily explained, gesturing with her hands.

"What?!" Jessica and Hope said together.

Stephen stirred on the couch but settled back down quickly.

"I've been on our parish council for a year now, since taking on my position as the principal of the parish school," Timothy began lowering his voice, "and at our last meeting, Father explained to the council members that he feels that by excluding people from Communion the Catholic Church is being intolerant. He informed us that he does not believe that Jesus would act in that manner."

"But Scripture?" Jessica began heatedly, sliding off the couch and into a sitting position on the floor.

Timothy and Lily shook their heads in unison, as he reached over and clasped Lily's fair hand gently in his own.

"The Parish council members have been trying to talk to one another independent of another meeting and determine what we feel is the best first step in addressing the situation," he explained.

"You need to go to the bishop!" Hope declared simply.

The room fell silent, everyone considering the gravity of the circumstance at St. Monica's and the impact this would have on the Warner household because of Timothy's position.

"Does Kelsey have a doctor yet?" Jessica asked Michael, turning in his direction and changing the subject.

"I have no idea," he responded.

"Well, I can give her the name of mine, but he's in Framingham," Jessica told him, leaning back against the sofa.

"Yeah, mine is in Worchester," Hope added.

"Michael, where does Kelsey live?" Lily asked.

Michael replied, "Catskill for school and Carlstown for home."

Lily thought for a moment and twirling one, long, dark curl on her finger said, "I don't know anyone who lives in either of those places that might know about a pro-life doctor there."

"Well, my mom is there," Michael reminded them.

"You should ask her about her doctor," Jessica said, pulling at the fabric of her orange tee.

Michael frowned slightly and Anna laughed.

"Well, you be sure to tell Kelsey that if anything gets crazy, she has plenty of places that she can stay," Hope told him.

"Yeah, I know that," he said, rubbing Hope's back briskly. "I'm so grateful. That's why I was hoping she could meet you guys tonight."

"One step at a time," Jessica said. "And I think she should meet Anna first, because she is closest to her age."

"What are you doing tomorrow?" Michael asked, turning to Anna. "Want to take a ride with me to Carlstown?"

She nodded and looked at her parents.

"Fine with me," Timothy told her.

"You're set with homework?" Lily asked Anna who

nodded her head.

"Actually, I have plenty myself," Michael said standing up and picking up his own chair. "I'm going to get out of here now and then I'll be back tomorrow so you and I can go to Carlstown." He quickly returned the chair to the dining room.

"I'll do some now," Anna assured her mother. "I don't have much."

"We should go too," Jessica said. Timothy offered his hand and helped to pull Jessica to her feet.

"Do you want to go to Church here or do you want to go to the teen Mass in Carlstown tomorrow about five?" Michael asked, returning to the room.

"Anna, I don't want you back too late tomorrow night," Timothy cautioned.

"I'll go to Mass here, with the family then," Anna responded.

Jessica pointed to the sleeping Stephen. "How am I gonna get him into the car?"

Michael said, "I'll carry him."

Hope took turns hugging Lily, Timothy and Michael, and then went into the other room to get her girls.

"It's so early," Rachel was protesting while walking to the front hall.

"Mom, do they have to go already?" Jane asked, following her friends around the corner.

"It's a much longer ride now," Hope was reminding them.

"That's the only bad thing about the new houses," Alicia was telling Zack.

"You kidding?" Zack asked. "I can't wait for you to leave."

He ducked quickly, but Alicia and Rachel both swatted him on opposite arms.

"Oof!" he exclaimed. "I'm only joking!" He and the two girls laughed.

"They'll be back soon," Lily promised Jane.

"We'll be back soon," Hope said at the same time.

This time everyone laughed. They started to put on their coats, taking turns hugging in the cramped front hall and Michael carried Stephen off to the car.

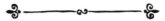

On his way back to Springfield, Michael called Kelsey to see if she had any plans for the next day. She was on the other line and did not pick up. He left her a message hoping that she was either telling Adam the news right then or talking to him to set up a time when they could meet.

His cell phone rang just as he was pulling into the parking lot at his apartment.

"Hi Kels," he said by way of greeting.

"Hi Michael." She sounded tired.

"You okay?" he asked, shutting off his car and leaning his head back against the headrest.

"Just tired... you?"

"Oh, I'm fine," he replied. "Listen, I'm calling because I really want to come down to Carlstown tomorrow and bring my friend, Anna, along to meet you."

"I don't want to feel like a specimen on display," she retorted, angrily.

"Kelsey, don't be like that," he told her. "Anna's my friend and she's a great girl. I just thought it might be nice for you to have someone who was more objective to talk to."

"I know what you're trying to do Michael," she told him.

"Look, I'm not bringing her down there to preach to you," he said. "I honestly just thought it might be easier for you to talk to someone you don't know as well as most of your other friends. You're so concerned about being judged by these people you don't know. Have you given any thought to what your "friends" are going to have to say about the situation?"

"Thanks," she said dryly.

"I'm not going to paint hearts and flowers for you Kelsey," he told her, raking his fingers through his hair. "It's situations like these that make you realize who your real friends truly are."

"I know," she said, suddenly quiet.

"So can I bring Anna down to meet you or not?" he pressed.

"Yeah…yeah, okay. You can bring Anna down to meet me," she replied.

"I'm telling you Kels – it'll be alright. You just have to trust me a little."

"Is there anything else?" she snapped.

"No, we'll probably be down just before lunch time," he said.

"Alright, see you then."

"Take it easy tonight, okay, Kels?" he suggested.

"I'm doing my best," she sighed.

"You're doing great! See you tomorrow then."

"Bye Michael."

"Good night."

CHAPTER THREE

Shifting Tides

Michael woke with a start early Sunday morning. His alarm clock had not even begun to ring. The sky outside his window was the gray dusk of early morning. As he lay in bed, staring up at the ceiling, he thought about Kelsey and her new baby. This kind of thing made him reflect back on the nephew that he did not know. It made him sad to consider it, but it gave him such peace to think that there was a little nephew of his, somewhere in the world. Sarah, his sister, had been just a freshman in college when she had gone into the city with her new college friends. Someone had laced her drink with Rohypnol, the date rape drug.

Michael lay in bed. He remembered that the time Sarah had been pregnant was the worst time for his family in so many ways. She was composed through the whole situation however, and she became frustrated with people who refused to understand why she had chosen to carry the baby to term. Her great faith made Michael feel weak and small in comparison — even now, so many years later. His nephew would be turning five this spring.

Looking over at the clock, Michael yawned. It was just past 6:30. If he went on like this for the next few days, he would never make it through his endless pile of schoolwork. Pulling the covers up around him, Michael squeezed his eyes shut and tried to make his brain stop thinking. It didn't work out; he ended up throwing off the covers and heading to the shower — envying his sleeping roommates even more than he usually did.

At ten o'clock in the morning, Michael walked down the center aisle of St. Monica's Church wearing navy pants and a white dress shirt. He slid into the pew next to Timothy Warner and the rest of the Warner clan. The two men shook hands and in moments, Lucy was scrambling up onto Michael's lap.

"Hey cutie," Michael whispered, kissing the top of Lucy's head. "You need to get down for a minute so I can say my prayers."

Lucy slid off of Michael's lap and stood resting her hand on his shoulder while he prayed with his head bowed and his hands clasped. Once he slid up and into the pew, she clamored back onto his lap. He smoothed her dress down over her little legs. Anna caught his eye and smiled at him shyly. Zack leaned over and gave him a vice-like handshake. Lily patted him on the arm as he shifted Lucy to his other leg. Jane gave a small wave from the end of the pew.

Everything about the Mass was familiar. The congregation sang the entrance hymn. The deacon and priest walked reverently to the altar. The Mass began with the Liturgy of the Word. When the Gospel reading, Luke 17: 5-10, was finished however, Father shut the Lectionary soundly and stood for a few moments looking out at his new congregation as they took their seats in one motion.

Lily Warner sat silently, watching the priest survey the room. She crossed her right leg over her left and then switched them quickly. Pulling her black woolen jacket tighter around her, she looked down to the floor, reciting a quick prayer to St. Michael.

Father leaned down to place the Lectionary on the shelf

beneath the pulpit. He stood erect and began his homily, like every other week, with parish announcements. After speaking about CCD activities, the next school fundraiser and the high school football team, he rubbed his hands together slowly.

Moving to grip the sides of the marble pulpit, Father began, "Dear Friends in Christ, I want first to thank you all for a very warm welcome to St. Monica's. I have been so well received this past month; it has been such a blessing. I don't know how many of you have ever considered the difficulties of being a priest. Leaving a parish is like leaving a family..."

He paused here and let these words settle before continuing. "Father Jeff was a wonderful, faithful priest for your parish family. He and I however, have a differing opinion in regards to the priorities of how a parish should run."

Timothy glanced at Lily and took his wife's hand. They both watched their new pastor closely. Michael looked from the priest at the pulpit to his friends sitting next to him and saw the discomfort clearly etched on their faces.

"There has been much discussion in recent days about tolerance in every aspect of our lives. As a priest, I truly believe that we need to consider this issue — even in terms of traditional religious practices. For that reason, I have made the decision to begin today to welcome all people to take part in our Holy Communion celebration."

A low murmur rippled through the congregation. Timothy and his wife shared a long, hard look. He shook his head slowly as her eyes began to fill with tears. In the moment of silence that followed this pronouncement, a father and mother sitting directly in front of them stood up suddenly, and taking their children by the hand, began to file quickly down the aisle. The wife cried openly as they went. Timothy watched over his shoulder, knowing this family had students at his school.

"I understand this change may be difficult for you to

accept," the pastor remarked sincerely, "but aren't all of the Church's teachings difficult?"

Lily tightened her grip on her husband's hand and looked at him with wide eyes. *What do we do?*

"The Eucharist is unchanging," he whispered softly, "the rest we will address after Mass."

Lily looked over at the surprised faces of her children, sitting there with her in the pew. Anna searched her mother's face. Their expressions reflected one another, remaining strong in the face of adversity. Zack raised his chin defiantly and was looking up at the crucifix hanging over the altar. Jane looked confusedly at the priest and then at the people sitting around her who were still whispering. Lucy, sitting on Michael's lap, seemed to sense that something quite serious was unfolding, as she remained still and did not fidget. She watched her parents with wide eyes.

Looking back to the pulpit, Lily heard the words the pastor spoke as if from far away and then more clearly as he continued, "...in this way, I hope to begin building a great bridge between our brothers and sisters of other faiths. I know that I can count on you to support your Pastor during this time of great change. God Bless you and God Bless America."

In the quiet moments after the homily, the people finished up their whispering as the pastor moved back to his seat. An uncomfortable silence filled the room and the congregation stood awkwardly to recite the Profession of Faith.

During the Liturgy of the Eucharist, the people were unusually reverent and solemn. Lily saw tears on the cheeks of both Michael and Timothy. Her heart welled up with anger as she knelt after receiving communion; how could this man, Christ's priest, be allowed to just change things?

She was distracted and upset. She wanted to experience the moment of Holy Communion as a solemn, reverent one and yet she could not even concentrate.

At the end of Mass, people congregated at the front of the church, out of the hearing range of the priest who was shaking hands with those leaving at the back. The Warners and Michael genuflected toward the tabernacle and then turned to walked quietly down the aisle. Anna was putting on her blue peacoat; Zack helped her into it. Jane stopped a moment to button up Lucy's long, red coat and the two of them walked quickly to catch up to the family. The Pastor was still standing just outside the doorway. He shook hands with each of the Warners except Lucy, who hung behind her mother. Timothy politely introduced him to Michael.

"Will I see you next week?" Father asked Timothy.

"I will be praying with my family about that," Timothy responded honestly. "I know that the Eucharist is unchanging, and I want to spiritually support the families in my school. I don't however, agree with what you are proposing to do at this parish."

"Michael, would you walk the children to the car?" Lily asked pointedly, placing Lucy's hand in his. Lily threaded her hand up and over her husband's arm and stood beside him in solidarity as they faced the pastor.

"Well, I'd like to thank you for all of your prayer support and all of your support with the school," Father continued.

"You'll still have all of our prayer support, Father," Lily assured him kindly. "I just don't know what we are going to do with the rest of this…"

Another family had come up the aisle and were waiting to the side to speak with Father. He shook hands briskly with Timothy and Lily and then turned his attention to the next group.

Michael had led Lucy down the steps of the church. She kept craning her neck to see what was happening between her parents and the priest. Anna, Zack and Jane had followed quietly behind.

Timothy and Lily held hands as they walked a short distance behind the children. They watched as Zack and Jane continued to laugh and joke for Lucy's sake. Lily studied Anna for a moment, proud that she was willing to go to Carlstown with Michael to help minister to Kelsey.

"We don't have to go today," Michael was saying as Lily and Timothy caught up to them, "if you'd rather not."

"Why?" Anna asked. "What difference will that make?"

Michael shrugged as Lucy peeked out from behind his leg. Zack jumped out from behind the van and made her squeal. Michael glanced at them distractedly. Everything had changed again, since morning Mass. This weekend had caused much upheaval in his world. He leaned back against the van.

"We need to go Michael," Anna was telling him. "You're gonna get your white shirt dirty."

He nodded his head and leaned away from the van. He knew she was right in both regards.

Anna and Michael turned to say goodbye to her family. She brushed off the back of his shirt gently. He felt his ears go pink and saw Jane looking at him curiously. He glanced away.

"I think going to Carlstown is even more important now than it was before," Lily told her daughter.

"Get in everyone," Timothy called in his deep baritone.

Anna nodded in agreement with her mother.

Timothy walked around the car getting everyone settled. He came around to Anna and gave his eldest a big hug. To Michael he said, "Drive safe. We'll talk more about this when you two return."

"See ya Mr. Warner."

Michael and Anna walked quickly to his car which was parked a short distance away. Michael opened the passenger door and held it while Anna got in. He shut it carefully, then rounded to his own side and got in.

Michael followed the van out of the parking lot and down the road as far as the highway entrance. He and Anna were going in one direction and the van was going in the other. Neither of them spoke at first, as he merged into traffic. They both seemed to be processing the reality of the homily that they had just heard.

"I honestly can't believe a priest would suggest sharing Communion with people who were not Catholic," Anna observed after a few moments. "Sure, he might operate that way, but why would he announce it publicly knowing that he might lose quite a number of his congregation?"

"I feel like I just entered an episode of the Twilight Zone," Michael said shaking his head.

"What do you think is going to happen now?" she asked him.

He shrugged.

"Do you think we should still go to that Church for Mass?"

"I don't know. Your father, as principal, has a hard call to make. As for me, I won't be going there again, " he replied.

"Did you get in touch with Kelsey last night? Is she even expecting us this afternoon?" Anna changed the subject.

"Yeah, I talked to her. She isn't thrilled, but I think she'll behave. I'm stopping by my house on the way. Are you cold?" Michael stretched his hand out to click on the heater.

"I'm okay," she replied. "How's your sister, Sarah?"

Anna thought of Michael's family and tucked a piece of her long, wavy hair behind her ear. Situations like this made everyone think of Sarah and the rest of his family. They had been through quite a lot over the past few years.

"She's doing well," Michael told her smiling. "She's been

dating Jason since she graduated from school. Perhaps there's something there."

Anna smiled and looked at her hands which were clasped in her lap. She was pleased for Sarah; she had met Jason just one time, but he seemed like a nice man.

"Do you want coffee?" Michael asked, stifling a big yawn.

"Nah, I'm good, but stop if you want something."

"I might have to. I feel like this weekend has lasted for the better part of my college life."

Anna laughed knowingly. "Yeah well, some situations are like that I'm afraid."

In another forty minutes, Michael was pulling his car into his parent's driveway. This was where he lived until he left for college and was nearby to Kelsey's house.

"I never did call my folks to tell them I'd be coming by," he told Anna as he turned to face her in the driveway. She smiled shyly.

They both got out and walked to the stairs leading up to the side deck. Anna heard Michael's family terrier barking on the other side of the door. The little grey dog was all wound up and running in circles in the kitchen. Michael let them in with his key since it didn't appear that anyone was home.

The dog yapped with joy when Michael bent down to stroke her short furry body.

"Maybe they had a coffee hour after Mass today," Michael observed. "Do you want a sandwich or something since we never stopped? It's about lunch time."

"That would be fine," Anna told him, shrugging out of her blue peacoat. "Whatever there is."

Michael stuck his head in the refrigerator as Anna bent down to pet the dog's sleek coat. "What's your dog's name again? I never remember."

"Angie," Michael replied, muffled from being in the

fridge. Anna could hear him moving some things around.

"Ham sandwich?" he asked, peering around the door.

"Great," Anna said, stroking Angie behind her floppy ears. The little dog nuzzled Anna's knees as she crouched on the floor.

Michael got the ham, bread, mayonnaise and cheese out of the fridge and put it onto the counter. He and Anna washed their hands in the kitchen sink. They were standing side-by-side, putting together their sandwiches when Michael's parents walked in the side door.

"Hey son," Patrick said happily, in his gruff voice. "I didn't know you would be here today."

Michael went around the kitchen island to give his father a big hug. Both men were the same height and clapped each other on the back soundly.

"Anna, it's so good to see you again!" Samantha exclaimed.

"Hello Mrs. Anderson," Anna said shyly. Michael's exuberant parents always made her feel a bit dowdy and she tugged on her flowered skirt self-consciously.

"Michael, what is going on with Kelsey?" his mother asked immediately, turning to look at him with her hands on her hips.

"Who did you see?" Michael asked her, "Her mom?"

"Yeah, Mrs. Springer was at Mass this morning and Kelsey wasn't with her. She let me know she was concerned about her daughter but said she was pleased because she was beginning to spend some time with you and not that boyfriend of hers," Samantha explained, gesturing with her hands. "I don't think she will ever forgive Kelsey for coloring that beautiful blonde hair of hers just because Adam preferred black…"

There was a sudden silence.

"Do you want sandwiches?" Anna offered.

"Thank you, but we just returned from brunch with our

friends," Patrick answered her.

"Yeah, Kelsey's got some things going on," Michael allowed, addressing his mother. He did not want to keep his parents in the dark but, he felt it only right that Kelsey be the one to share her news with the wider world.

"Well, it's good then she has a friend like you to talk to," Patrick told him, patting his back.

Anna packed up the leftover ham, bread, mayonnaise and cheese and began putting them into the fridge taking as much time as she could. Michael carried their plates over to the small breakfast nook as his parents took their leave of the kitchen.

"That was a bit awkward," Michael confessed as Anna joined him at the small table. "Shall we pray?"

They bowed their heads and said the blessing before beginning to eat.

"Do you want soda?" Michael asked as he put down his half-eaten sandwich.

"Sure, that would be fine, thank you," Anna replied, dabbing her lips with a paper napkin.

Michael returned to the fridge. "Ginger Ale, okay?" he asked over his shoulder.

"Sure."

Michael brought two cans of ginger ale to the table, opening one and handing it to Anna.

"Thanks."

"So after we eat, I'll call Kelsey and let her know we're down here," Michael said, sliding back onto the chair. "Then we can figure out what she wants to do. Maybe we can meet at the bookstore."

"Something like that would probably be best," Anna agreed, sipping from her soda. "Whatever we do, it's bound to be tense."

Michael nodded in agreement and began to fold back the cuffs of his white shirt.

"How are things going with your folks?" Anna asked quietly.

"Well, they still don't really support what I'm doing for school. My dad thinks I need to go to a real school so I can get a real job. He doesn't see youth ministry as a real job…especially in light of everything going on in the Church these days."

"He might not be that far off the mark," Anna suggested, "between parish priorities and today's economy, there might not be that much youth work available."

Michael nodded and swallowed. "I just don't know what else to do now. I've thought about maybe transferring to St. Francis in Ohio."

"Really?" Anna asked surprised. "That's actually my first choice."

"They have real degrees over there in many fields; not just theology like where I am now. I'm thinking that might ease my father's mind a bit."

Anna nodded thoughtfully, chewing a bite of her sandwich. "What do your parents want you to do?"

"Well, my dad has always hoped that I would follow in his footsteps and become a scientist. I have to admit that I'm really interested in genetic engineering," Michael replied wiping his mouth with the back of his hand. "And my mom just wants me to get a job with good pay so I can settle down and give her some grandchildren."

Anna laughed. It was a light, fresh sound that brought a smile to Michael's face.

"Where are your parents with the whole college thing?" he asked in return.

"I know they are thrilled that I'm interested in St. Francis," she told him, "but with the direction that the Church is taking…

and you know, all that stuff about the Mayan calendar and the end of civilization..."

Michael and Anna laughed together.

"I know my dad is worried about me being that far away," she concluded.

"I can understand that. Have you looked into any schools closer to home?"

"Yeah, Christ's Kingdom in New Hampshire... I don't think it's what I'm looking for though," she replied, "Too formal."

Michael nodded in agreement and took the last bite of his sandwich. Immediately his cell phone rang.

"Kelsey," he said with a mouthful. He turned away and mumbled "Hello," into the mouthpiece.

Anna laughed and popped the last bite of her sandwich into her mouth. She got up to clear the table and give Michael a moment to talk. She stacked the dishes in the sink and then retrieved the empty soda cans. She rinsed them for the recycling bin and placed them on the counter, then she knelt down to give some attention to Angie who had heard the sound of dishes being cleared and came to investigate.

"I'm sorry kiddo," Anna said scratching the dog behind her floppy ears, "it's all gone."

Angie looked at her with large puppy eyes. Still talking on the phone, Michael pointed to a cabinet in the island and there Anna found some dog treats. She gave one to Angie who sat up on her hind legs to get it.

"What a pretty girl!" Anna told her.

Angie downed the treat and then trotted back out of the room at the same time Michael hung up the phone.

"Kelsey sounds upset," he told her. I'm wondering if she's spoken to Adam or to her mom..."

"Is this a good time then?" Anna asked, coming out from

behind the kitchen island.

"Yeah, we're going to meet at the bookstore I was telling you about."

Anna nodded and grabbed her purse which was hanging over the back of the chair.

"Let me tell my folks we're leaving," Michael said. He left the room and headed down the stairs in the direction of the family room. He was followed back up the stairs by both of his parents who were talking at the same time.

"Don't wait so long to come back," Michael's father chided in his guff voice.

"It was good to see you again, Mr. Anderson," Anna told him, shaking his outstretched hand firmly.

Samantha Anderson leaned over to give Anna a quick hug. "Please give our regards to your parents," she said.

"I certainly will, Mrs. Anderson," Anna replied. "Take care everyone. I hope to see you again soon."

Michael helped Anna into her coat. He escorted her out of the house and down to his car where he opened the passenger door before she could get to it.

Anna laughed. "Thanks for being so old-fashioned," she told him. "Your light years ahead of most of the guys I know."

He shut her in, smiling to himself, and in a few moments, they were driving out of the driveway and back down the road towards the bookstore they had passed on their way to the house.

———————◆———————

Kelsey had not arrived by the time they reached the bookstore. Michael and Anna got a table in the cafe area that was a bit out of the way and ordered their drinks. They were just beginning to sip them when Kelsey came in.

Anna watched her as she scanned the room. The wisp of a girl standing just inside the doorway was as pale as death with severe black hair pulled back in a messy pony. She wore jeans with a rip on one knee, a white cami and an over sized black hoodie that zipped up. Her hazel eyes looked tired and just as they came to rest on Michael, Anna got up quickly, ducking her head and left for the bathroom. She and Michael had agreed that she would give him just a moment to access the situation; to try to help Kelsey to be more comfortable in meeting Anna. They were working hard to make it seem more like a friendly meeting and less like an ambush. They were sensitive of Kelsey, especially in her heightened emotional state.

When Anna came out of the bathroom, she could see that Kelsey was crying, but not hysterical. She hesitated for another moment and then walked cautiously over to the table. She remembered Kelsey from a couple of youth events she had attended. Michael had convinced Kelsey to help a time or two. Anna could see what Kelsey's mom had against the black hair — it made her look almost sickly. Of course, the emotion of the past few weeks was a major contributing factor to that as well.

As Anna slid into the empty chair between Kelsey and Michael, Kelsey looked at her warily. She took in Anna's pretty appearance and made no secret of sizing her up.

"Hi Kelsey," Anna said softly, brushing her dark hair behind her ears. "I remember you from some of the activities that Michael would plan for the youth group. You often helped out at them."

Kelsey regarded her with interest for a moment. "Really?" she said airily, "I don't remember you at all."

Anna did not respond to the jibe. Kelsey continued to size her up and then looked away. Anna remained quiet, watching Kelsey. Michael set his jaw. He opened his mouth to speak, but Anna shook her head.

"So then what did Adam say?" Michael prodded, without

wasting any more time.

"Nothing I could repeat in a family-friendly bookstore," Kelsey responded, turning to look back at him coolly.

Michael shook his head. "I had hoped he could be a little more reasonable, especially if what you told me about him yesterday was true."

Kelsey looked at Anna accusingly. "So how much do you know?"

"All the important parts," Anna replied simply. "As for Adam, I'm sure he's just as scared as you are."

Kelsey remained silent. Her cold hazel eyes regarding Anna steadily.

"I sure as heck would be," Michael offered, to keep the conversation moving.

"So what's this meeting all about anyway?" Kelsey asked brusquely. She gazed at Michael waiting for a response.

"I just wanted you to know that you could contact me if you needed someone to talk to."

Anna spoke softly and kindly to Kelsey, who still wasn't paying her any attention. Anna took out a piece of paper from her purse. It was an old receipt from the grocery store. She scrawled her phone number and email on the backside of it quickly.

"Sometimes it helps to have a more objective opinion; especially when your friends start to write you off." She slid the slip of paper in Kelsey's direction.

Kelsey looked at her angrily, her pale skin drawn tight around her eyes. "How would you know what my friends are gonna do?!"

"You aren't the first person I've known in this situation," Anna replied softly. "Have you even told any of your friends yet?"

Kelsey looked from her to Michael with a pained

expression.

"Well, you two know... not that you count." She pointed dramatically at Anna. "And Adam now. I think my room mate might suspect something but we haven't actually discussed it yet."

"When do you go back?" Michael asked her, pushing up the cuffs of his white shirt.

"After this fantastic little meeting," she said dryly.

"What kind of person is Adam?" Anna asked with interest.

Her quiet and kind demeanor threw Kelsey off balance. "He's the quiet type. Why?"

"Does he have a hot temper?"

"Sometimes," Kelsey replied honestly.

"It would probably be a good idea for you not to be alone with him right now," Anna suggested.

Kelsey did not reply. She had not even considered what it would be like when she returned to school and had to be with Adam again. She ran a shaking hand absently up her arm.

Michael was nodding his head. "Yeah, Anna's right. You make sure that you talk with him only in public places for the time being. You need to really be able to judge his reaction to this news."

Kelsey looked from Michael to Anna.

"You're scaring me," she confessed, placing a trembling hand on the table.

"We don't want to scare you," Anna stressed kindly. "We just want you to really think about what you are doing the next few days. An unplanned pregnancy is probably the most possible tension that any one relationship can endure."

"I hadn't thought much about that," Kelsey replied resigned.

"Look," Michael told her, his tone all business. "For now,

I want you to check in with Anna or I twice a day – mornings and night."

"Okay, I'll send you a text."

"Not good enough," Anna said, leaning toward her and gazing into those deep hazel eyes. "You need to call so we can actually hear your voice."

Kelsey puzzled at this request and then nodded with comprehension. "You don't think…"

Michael shook his head quickly. "No, I don't… but it's always better to be safe than sorry. And besides that, you need to tell one of your friends on campus — just in case there's an emergency. How about your room mate?"

Kelsey looked thoughtful for a moment. "Can I tell my Chem. Professor?"

"You can tell anyone you want, Kelsey," Michael told her, "but one of your friends needs to know — best if it's someone you tend to hang out with. Your Chem. Professor won't be going with you guys to the movies or to a party."

Kelsey nodded her head. "Yeah, okay. I get it."

"And then you need to call me every morning," Michael said, placing his hand over her trembling one.

She agreed.

"And me in the evening," Anna reminded her.

She nodded to that too.

"Thoughts about a doctor?" Anna asked, throwing all caution to the wind.

Kelsey gave her a long, hard look. The veil seemed to snap back over her hazel eyes. When she responded, her tone was even.

"I'm still considering my options."

Anna nodded in understanding. She took a moment and prayed a silent prayer.

"Well, I've got some good friends back home, they are

both older single moms..."

"The ones that Michael knows?" Kelsey interrupted.

Anna nodded. As she talked to Kelsey, she realized how much she knew about being a single mother because the whole family had been so close to Hope and Jessica during their individual family struggles.

"They each have good doctor referrals for you, but they are up in our area. You really need to make an appointment and get a check up."

Kelsey shivered. She clutched her black hoodie closed over her chest.

"I'll see if I can talk to them about finding out about a doctor closer to where you go to school," Anna suggested.

Kelsey shook her head. "No, I'd rather go somewhere up your way."

"Kelsey," Michael said, putting his hand on her shoulder. "This week is going to be really horrible for you."

"Thanks," she said dryly, looking away.

"Look, I told you before that I'm going to give it to you straight." He let go of her. "All this will work out and you know what the best option is for both you and your baby. Don't make any crazy decisions because you are afraid. If you are afraid or going to do something stupid, you call one of us up and we'll come down there and bring you somewhere you can think."

Kelsey nodded her head as her eyes swam with tears.

"Chelsea's Choice won't give you the kind of help that you really need," Anna said softly.

Kelsey looked at her pointedly. "Who really knows what's best for me but me?" she shot.

"I can give you statistic after statistic, but that won't really help you Kelsey," Anna replied softly. "I can see in your eyes that you know we are telling you the truth. You really need to step out in faith on this one. Michael really cares about you and so do I. The best thing you can do right now when you are hurting and confused is to trust the people who really care about what's best for you in the long run."

Kelsey dropped her eyes and looked at the floor. One tear made it's way down her cheek and she brushed it away angrily.

"Not the people who want to help you to make a hasty decision that you will live to regret all of your life," Anna continued. "You have already been changed by this pregnancy, Kelsey. There will never be a time again when you can take this back. Don't do something that will make this difficult situation become something you will second guess yourself for, for the rest of your life. No one should have to deal with this alone and you won't have to, I promise. But you have to be strong and do what's best for both of you. Don't let anyone scare you into making any decisions. You can have all the time and support that you need."

Michael, who had sat back to let Anna do the talking, leaned forward. He regarded Anna thoughtfully for a few moments, thanking God that she was here and a part of his life.

"That's the real reason I wanted you to meet Anna, Kelsey," he told her.

Kelsey looked up to meet his eyes.

"Because she already cares about you, even more than any of the people you call your friends. That's just the kind of person that she is."

Kelsey's eyes filled up again with tears. "I'm scared!" Her breathing came fast and shallow.

"I know you are. And it makes sense that you would be, but you don't have to let it overwhelm you," Anna told her, rubbing her back gently.

The three sitting at the table fell silent for a time as Kelsey took a few deep breaths and Anna continued to rub her back.

"Are you driving back right from here?" Michael asked

finally.

"Yeah," Kelsey replied, drying her eyes with the back of her hand and shaking off Anna's hand in annoyance.

"How long will it take?"

"Just under an hour," she replied.

"Be careful, okay?" Anna asked. "Are you sure you're all right to drive?"

Kelsey took another deep breath. "Life won't stop a moment to let me get off so I guess I just need to keep at it."

The three of them stood at the same time, the sound of their chairs a loud scraping in the quiet cafe.

"Let me get you a hot chocolate for the road," Michael suggested, moving around the table to head to the register.

"And water," Anna reminded him.

He walked over to the counter while the girls walked to the door and stood talking for a few more minutes.

"Let me know you got in okay," Anna was telling Kelsey as Michael handed Kelsey the small hot chocolate and a bottle of water.

He opened the door, letting them both pass and they all walked over to Kelsey's car. She placed the drinks on her roof and turned to hug Michael tightly, burying her head in his chest for a moment. He stroked her hair comfortingly.

When they broke apart, Anna reached out to hug her, but Kelsey quickly extended her hand. Anna took it gently and shook it, giving her a friendly squeeze.

"Come see us next weekend," Michael told her.

Kelsey looked them over thoughtfully and Anna started to laugh. "No," she said, "he's not my boyfriend. We just have a lot of mutual friends and tend to see each other pretty frequently."

Kelsey nodded but eyed them suspiciously.

"But if you do come up this weekend, I can introduce you

to the friends I was telling you about," Anna told her, folding her arms tightly over her chest.

Kelsey nodded. "I'll let you know."

Michael and Anna walked back to his car and watched Kelsey drive smoothly out of the parking lot.

Anna sat down in the passenger seat and a moment later she was crying quietly.

"You okay?" Michael asked gently, putting the car back into park.

She nodded her head, digging through her purse for a kleenex. Michael turned on the music just a little bit to let Anna process whatever she was thinking about without any interference from him.

CHAPTER FOUR
Reality Check

When Michael and Anna returned to her house just past six o'clock that evening, they were not at all surprised to see a bunch of cars parked along the street. Anna picked out the ones that she recognized. There seemed to be an abundance of friends and a couple of the priests from the area who were also friends of the family.

"Do you want to come in?" Anna asked, as Michael pulled the car to a stop in the Warner's driveway.

"Who's over?" he asked, looking around at all the vehicles.

"I think they've called in the cavalry," she told him. "From what I can tell it just might be that every VIP in the area is here to consult about what our priest said this morning at Mass."

"I have so much work to do," he ruminated. "But you know what; this is an evening I just can't miss."

He shifted the car into park and the two of them got out quickly.

Anna pushed open the front door. It was unlocked.

Immediately to the left, the group had gathered in the living room and dining room areas of the house. A discussion was already underway. Anna walked opposite the group, down

68

the short hall and peeked into the family room. The rest of the kids must be playing in the basement. She shrugged out of her peacoat and hung it over the back of the wing-back chair. She led Michael through the kitchen and around into the dining room. Timothy motioned for them to pull up chairs. Since there was not much room, the two just moved over to a corner in the dining room where they could watch the discussion unfold. They stood together up against the wall. No one else seemed to notice that they had arrived.

Fr. Larry, an older, slightly overweight priest with salt and pepper hair who was still wearing his clerics was speaking heatedly.

"So what do we do then? Just let anyone who wants Holy Communion take His body and blood even if they don't even believe in it."

"Hold on folks, offenses against orthodoxy and traditional Catholic practices are nothing new since Vatican II. I think you just ought to pull out and come to my Church." Fr. Jeff said, his youthful face breaking into a sympathetic grin.

Everyone laughed.

Timothy however, still looking serious, replied, "That's fine for the rest of my family but remember, I'm principal of the High School a block from St. Monica's as well as being a lector there. Don't you think my absence will be noticed?"

Zack brightened up suddenly, "Hey, that means I can play on Mark's CYO team if we go to Sacred Heart instead."

Lily joined in, her brow creased in thought. "Not so fast there Zack, I don't think the family should separate for Sunday Mass."

Zack scowled, his dreams of a basketball championship going up in flames.

Fr. Jeff, wearing a NY Giants team jersey over his clerics, stated calmly, "In my parish, I always put an announcement in the program for funerals, weddings, baptisms and confirmations, explaining who should present themselves for Communion. This information is also listed on the back page of the Sunday Missal we have in the pews."

"We need to stop and think about how the Church has survived all this time in Communist China," Fr. John Mary suggested in his quiet voice. "Remember, nothing will prevail against it. Even a priest with a misguided sense of what is right."

Fr. John Mary was the only priest in the room from an order. As a member of the Franciscian Friars of the Renewal, he wore the usual gray tunic and rope belt.

"Communist China?" Jessica murmured quietly, cradling Stephen who was asleep in her arms, mouth wide open, with a peaceful expression on his baby-face.

Michael and Anna looked at one another. Then Anna turned and looked at all the people gathered in the two rooms with her brown eyes wide. An underground Catholic church like in China…the idea was as foreign to her as 45 rpm record singles. Zack got up from his seat then and motioned for Anna to take it; he moved back into the corner with Michael. The two guys stood, backs up against the wall and arms crossed over their chests.

Anna sat down between her friend Alicia, Hope's oldest daughter, and Jessica. Jessica took her hand and gave it a quick squeeze.

"Did you meet Kelsey?" Jessica whispered, leaning in to speak quietly just to Anna.

Alicia leaned in from Anna's other side because for her, Kelsey was the more important of the two situations.

Anna nodded. "So far we're doing okay with that one."

"I'm so glad," Alicia breathed. "Rachel and I fasted all day."

"I'll tell you more later," Anna said quietly.

Jessica, Anna and Alicia turned their attention back to the on-going discussion.

"What do we do next Sunday then?" Zack challenged.

"Has anyone talked to Fr. Sullivan?" Michael asked. "As rector of Our Lady of Guadalupe College and Seminary, he could be a natural to ask about this situation. I'm sure he'd know whether you guys have to leave in protest now that the new pastor has laid down the gauntlet, or whether you have to stay and grin and bear it because of the job."

Timothy stood up, hands on his back to stretch out the stress, and said, "I already put in a call to him. He's my spiritual director."

Lily pleaded, "Please pray a novena to St. Jude for us." Sensing people were getting ready to leave, she continued quickly,"We're also going to activate our usual crisis pregnancy prayer chain for Michael's friend. Please, stick around for coffee. Janey and I made a whole batch of brownies before that wonderful girl agreed to babysit in the basement."

Hope and Jessica, who were in charge of the prayer chain, went to the dining room table to draw up a quick schedule and make some phone calls. Lily began passing out mugs of steaming coffee.

Timothy stopped his wife as she was heading back into the kitchen and asked the three priests to say a prayer over them that they might do the will of God in this difficult situation. Lily and Timothy bowed their heads, holding hands, as Fr. John Mary said a few quiet words of blessing.

After making the sign of the cross together, Timothy leaned over and kissed his wife on the cheek tenderly. He squeezed her hands one last time. When he let them go, she returned to the kitchen.

Once Lily left earshot, Fr. Jeff muttered to Fr. Larry, "So it will just be one big Eucharistic free-for-all at St. Monica's then?"

"There have been people saying for years that the church has no right to deny anyone from receiving communion," Fr. Larry responded grimly.

"And how many abuses has that novelty perpetrated?" Timothy asked rhetorically, shaking his head slowly.

Lily joined them with her own steaming mug and lamented, "There will no longer be anything that sets us apart from the world, there will no longer be anything sacred."

"The Eucharist will remain sacred," Fr. John Mary reminded them. "It will just become a scandal in the process."

"So as the news gets out, St. Monica's might become bigger and more liberal, but the smaller, more conservative parishes, like mine, will remain," Fr. Jeff pointed out, "because for most people it's really about hedging their bets in case Hell is real after all. Most of the flock hasn't gotten the message of the Eucharist for years."

Hope and Jessica returned to the room with a schedule full of people willing to pray for Kelsey.

"Thank you for the coffee," Fr. Larry was saying to Lily, "but I really must be going."

Timothy took the empty cup from Fr. Larry and placed it on the coffee table.

Lily stood on tiptoe and hugged her friend. "Thank you for all of your prayers, Father."

"I should go as well," said Fr. John Mary, handing off his mug and offering Lily his hand.

She shook it firmly. "Thank you too, Father. Your prayer support really means a great deal to us."

The priests said their goodbyes and took their leave of the cozy Warner home.

"Do you plan to call the Bishop's office on what this new pastor is up to?" Fr. Jeff was asking, as the door shut behind Fr. John Mary.

Timothy sighed. "I haven't figured that out yet."

"How about a Rosary?" Hope suggested.

"Zack, please call the kids up from downstairs," Timothy instructed.

Anna's cell phone rang. She looked down at her phone and to Michael she nodded. To her father, she said, "Kelsey — gotta take it."

Timothy nodded as Anna quickly left the room, talking softly into the phone. The rest of the kids clamored up the stairs and were weaving around the grownups looking for places to settle in to pray. In another moment, Anna was sliding back into her seat.

"Everything all set?" Michael asked.

She nodded, pushing a strand of hair behind her ear and clasping her hands lightly on her lap.

"What a wonderful group to pray with," Fr. Jeff remarked smiling, as he raised his hand to make the Sign of the Cross.

The gathering broke up once the recitation of the Rosary had ended. Everyone left except for Hope and her daughters, Alicia and Rachel. Michael had to try to salvage some of his coursework that had been neglected all weekend. Jessica and Stevie went too since she had to get up early for work. She and Hope had driven in separate cars this time. Lily sent her younger girls and Zack upstairs to get ready for the week and for the littlest one, Lucy, to change into pajamas.

"How did your meeting go with Kelsey?" Lily asked her eldest, Anna, as they settled into the family room to decompress.

"I think it went pretty well actually," Anna observed, smoothing down her flowered skirt. "Initially she was beastly, but after that, she mellowed out some."

"She must really be scared to death," Hope remarked, fiddling with her hair which had been pulled back into a french braid. She and her daughters had joined Lily and Anna in the family room.

"I guess she talked to her boyfriend and that didn't go over very well," Anna explained.

"Is she back at school now?" Rachel asked with concern.

"Yeah, Michael set up a daily call pattern – she needs to check in with each of us regularly. We want to make sure she is okay and isn't going to do something rash. She's pretty early on so I think we've been able to assure her that she has some time to make her decision – she doesn't need to rush into anything," Anna explained.

"That's such a great idea," Rachel observed, pulling the elastic out of her long, dark hair and letting it flow down her back.

"Is she open to having the baby?" Alicia asked, absently chewing on her fingernail.

"It seems so right now," Anna replied, crossing her legs and leaning back into the wing-back chair. "Michael never made it seem like she had committed to any decision. My impression is that we just need to guide her in the right direction."

Lily nodded thoughtfully. "I don't think anyone really wants to make the decision to have an abortion. I just don't think they have any idea what to do… it seems like a problem solver."

Heads were bobbing in agreement.

"How are you feeling about the new pastor and his decision?" Hope asked looking at her friend with concern.

"Honestly, I feel like the rug has been pulled right out from under me," Lily told her, putting a hand to her forehead. "Initially today I wanted to just get up and walk out. The family seated in front of us did just that. I was all set to follow them. It took Tim reminding me that it was still the Eucharistic Lord who I would encounter there."

"But what this Pastor is doing can't be allowed by Rome,

can it?" Alicia asked, leaning forward and putting her elbows on her knees.

"I wonder what Rome really knows of the goings on over here in America," Lily remarked. "It doesn't seem possible to me that they would accept such an overall invitation. That's very different than a priest using his own judgment about some stranger coming up for Holy Communion."

"I can't wait to see what the Bishop says... that is, if Timothy asks him," Hope stated.

The women sat quietly for a few moments.

"Well," said Hope standing up, "we really need to get going. Our holy hour for Kelsey is scheduled for three am. I'd like to get back and settle in for a couple of hours anyway."

Hope and Lily took a quick walk around to collect the remaining coffee mugs. All of the kids came back downstairs to say good-bye to their friends. Hope and her girls went into the living room to say good bye to Timothy and Zack who were on the sofa having a debate about the following Sunday.

"Drive safe," Timothy told her after giving her and the girls a big hug. He and Zack walked them to the door.

"See you guys," Hope said. She and her daughters waved to the Warners and walked down the silent street lit by the neighbor's outside lights.

Michael's cell phone woke him up again on Monday morning. It was Kelsey calling to check in; she sounded fairly upbeat. He wondered as he hung up if she had just moved into denial phase.

Setting up his schedule to avoid all classes until ten in the morning was supposed to allow Michael some much needed time to sleep in. Phone calls at eight thirty however, ruined those best laid plans. Now that he was awake, he had the sudden impulse to make a real breakfast. Both of his roommates had already left; neither of them was still in school. The youngest of the brothers he lived with had just graduated in May. Michael had met them through a group of friends at the Young Adult group and it was the answer to his prayer that they had stayed in the apartment after graduation. It had allowed him to remain enrolled in school. If he had to drive daily from Carlstown, he never would have been able to afford to continue there.

Michael arrived on time for his ten-thirty class wearing clean jeans and a collared shirt. His professor, Fr. Sullivan, the rector, took a jibe at priests who gave out communion to Protestants. This he equated to an "American Catholic Church" and said it would be a marker to usher in the end of the world.

Michael wondered if Timothy Warner had already spoken to him about the new pastor's dissenting views. He considered asking the rector whether Fr. Sullivan thought, under such circumstances, lay people should report a priest to the Bishop. As Father didn't welcome questions that did not deal with the material at hand, Michael knew he would need to wait until the end of class.

As soon as class was over, the room emptied out and Michael stayed to accompany Fr. Sullivan to the refectory to get his input on the Warner's situation.

"Father Sullivan, I was curious... as a layman, if I happened to hear a priest preaching about giving communion to Protestants, would I be responsible to call the Bishop's office to report him?"

The Rector stopped in his tracks and studied Michael carefully. Then Fr. Sullivan stated, "If the Bishop is as good as ours is, definitely, but it would have to be done directly, not through the office staff. That could give rise to gossip and scandal."

Michael nodded his head in understanding and went over to stand in the lunch line.

In the refectory, Michael sat with a group of seminarians from the order of St. Sebastian. "Guys, I need you to pray for a friend of mine — Kelsey. She just found out she's pregnant."

The table of young men dressed in black cassocks focused their attention on Michael.

"Is there any way we can help?" Br. Andrew asked him plainly concerned. Br. Andrew was one of the youngest seminarians there and tended to wear his feelings on his sleeve.

"Prayers mainly," Michael replied between mouthfuls of food.

"Have you taken her to the pro-life women's center?" Br. Gregory asked sensibly, cocking his head to the side.

"Well, it's a bit complicated," Michael explained. "She's in school in New York but her family's address is in Carlstown where she was home for the weekend."

The brothers nodded.

"Is she committed to having the baby?" Br. Gregory asked.

"I don't know," Michael told them, setting down his glass of milk. "I like to believe that with enough support she will see it through."

"That's why she needs a place like St. Gianna's," Br. Jonathan told him, fork hanging in the air. "They'll be there every day until she has the baby."

"She's not ready yet," Michael said. "In fact, I don't even think her parents know yet."

"Yes but, does the father?" Br. Gregory asked.

Michael nodded.

"And how did that go?"

"Not well, but not horrible, I guess," Michael answered, "And I've already got Jessica and Hope in the loop."

The brothers nodded their heads knowingly. Both of the single moms had taken courses at the school over the past few years and were pretty well known by the staff and students there.

"Hey, I've gotta get to class," Br. Jonathan said hurriedly, looking up at the clock.

All as one, the seminarians at the table stood and prayed in Thanksgiving, Michael with them.

"Catch up with you guys later," Br. Jonathan said, grabbing his books from where they were piled up on the floor.

"Go on," Br. Andrew told him motioning toward the door. "I've got this." He began stacking Br. Jonathan's dirty dishes on his own tray.

"Thanks," Br. Jonathan called over his shoulder.

Michael's cell phone rang. It was his father. It was unusual that his father would phone him during the day. Br. Andrew looked at him questioningly.

"Hey Dad, is everything okay?" Michael asked by way of greeting.

Br. Andrew nodded and started stacking Michael's dishes as well.

Michael waved a silent thank you to his friend and walked out the door, leaving his things at the table. He went to stand under the overhang edging the old building.

"Hey Son. I wanted to check in and see how things were going?" his father's gruff voice explained. "I heard through the grapevine that the new pastor at St. Monica's shocked the congregation over the weekend with his new plan for the parish. People as far away as here have been talking about it. That didn't actually happen, did it?"

"Yeah, I was there when he said it. The Warners are pretty shook up. They might leave the parish, but it's complicated since Mr. Warner is principal at the high school."

Patrick replied, "Well, when you see them, be sure to tell them they're more than welcome at our parish. By the way, I bumped into Kelsey at the Mobile station. She looked strange, maybe dizzy… she isn't pregnant, is she?"

"Yeah," Michael said simply, leaning back against the wall.

His father was silent a moment. "Did you have anything to do with this?"

"Are you kidding me?!" Michael exclaimed loudly, standing up straight and taking a few angry steps forward.

"It's in a father's nature to want to know these things," Patrick responded.

"You are seriously going to ask me that?" Michael demanded.

"Okay, look," Patrick began in a placating tone, "I'm not trying to offend you... "

"You're doing a damn good job!" Michael kicked at a small rock.

"Michael, listen to me," Patrick said, "the researchers in my office have been following trends in teen pregnancy for some time."

"So?" Michael remarked impatiently, "I thought the numbers were going down."

"Well, that's just it," Patrick replied, "They were going down. They were going down for quite a number of years. All of a sudden, in the past few months, the numbers have been beginning to skyrocket again. We don't believe this is a coincidence."

"What does that have to do with Kelsey?" Michael asked frowning.

"I'm not sure," Patrick said honestly, "but the strangest thing is that it seems to be happening in clusters."

Michael was silent for a few minutes. "So what you are telling me is that there are clusters of girls all getting pregnant all at the same time?"

"Yeah, that's what I'm saying," his father responded.

"Isn't that strange?" Michael asked.

"We think so," Patrick replied.

"What do you think is going on?"

"I have no idea," Patrick said, "but I do think something is going on."

"Can I do something?" Michael asked, softening his attitude toward his father.

"Just try to get Kelsey to the doctor as soon as you can, ok?"

"That's the plan," Michael said, "I'll call you if I have any more information."

"Great son. And I'm sorry that I asked about your involvement with that whole situation," Patrick told him.

Michael mumbled a reply and then hung up.

Michael called Anna's cell on his way home after his classes were done for the day, but she did not pick up. Perhaps she was working, or the family was having dinner. He thought about calling Mr. Warner directly to see if Fr. Sullivan had advised him to report the new pastor to the Bishop, but he had lost so much time over the weekend he knew he needed to pay some attention to his schoolwork. Getting involved in another phone conversation that would raise his blood pressure wouldn't help him to concentrate.

"Hey there," Hope said to Lily, "I'm getting ready to leave work and I just wanted to know if it would be worth it to travel back out your way this evening in case Timothy was advised to call the Bishop and you needed prayer support for your decision?"

"I've no word from Tim," Lily told her. "Let me give him a call and I'll let you know what I hear."

"Okay, sounds great," Hope said, phone resting on her

shoulder while she shuffled through a stack of files on her desk.

"I mean, I like you guys and all, but the time in the car is beginning to get to me."

"Oh no, I totally understand," Lily told her, laughing, "I'll call you back."

As soon as she hung up, Hope got a text from Rachel – going to Jane's?

Hope hit the call number and let Rachel know that there seemed to be no news yet; when she knew, she'd let the girls know.

Her phone beeped so she switched over to the incoming call from Lily.

"Still no word," Lily told her.

"Is that strange?" Hope asked, grabbing her purse and switching off the light in her office.

"I don't know," Lily responded. "Tim didn't say much else."

"Alright, well in that case, I think we're going to remain at the homestead… you be sure to call me though if you need anything."

"Will do," Lily assured her.

"I'm sure we'll be seeing you sooner rather than later," Hope told her shutting and locking the office door.

"I'm counting on it. Have a good night."

"You too."

Jessica called in then to see what Hope's evening plans were. The girls had gotten Stevie off of the bus and Jessica had no plans for the night. Hope let her know that they could have dinner together this evening. Jessica would stop to get some milk. The conversation ended just as Hope was getting into the driver's seat.

The drive home was uneventful. Road construction was causing a bit of a back up so it took Hope longer than usual.

When she arrived, Jessica was already home and dinner was cooking at her house. It was almost ready.

Hope stopped at home to unload her things and then went directly to Jessica's. She helped with the table chores and in just a few minutes, both families were sitting down to a nice dinner of chicken and rice.

Everyone was chattering around the table.

Stevie started to hum, to get everyone's attention.

"Oh, I'm sorry, Stephen," Jessica said, turning her attention to him. "Did you want to tell us how your day at school was? I'm sorry, go ahead."

Stephen looked around the table and then turned directly to Rachel. He cocked his head and looked up into her eyes. He began to moan and hum loudly. Since he had no words, this was his language.

"Really, that's so funny!" Rachel told him, taking both of his hands in hers and giggling.

"Aaahhh, aaahhh, ummmm," Stevie explained.

"And did you get in trouble for that?" Rachel coached.

Stephen quieted immediately and seemed to consider what Rachel had asked him. He grinned his winning smile and raised his hand for yes.

"You are such a trouble maker!" Alicia laughed, shaking him gently.

Stephen laughed with her and then turned in her direction. He bowed his head to her cheek giving her a Stevie kiss.

Jessica watched this exchange between her son and Hope's girls with a small smile on her face. She felt so grateful that God had given her the gift of being Stephen's mother. Hope caught her eye and they shared a knowing glance. It really wasn't true, as the abortion propaganda would have it, that children with disabilities would be better off never to have been born.

Chapter Five
The Gauntlet

On **Wednesday, Michael decided** he would like to connect with Kelsey and see if they could meet up that evening. He wanted to see how she was doing personally.

After finishing the first draft of the paper that had been hanging over his head since the weekend, Michael looked at the clock. It was just after four o'clock in the afternoon. He flipped open his cell phone and placed a call to Kelsey.

She picked up on the first ring.

"Hey Michael," she said sounding tired.

"Hi Kelsey; whatcha doin?" he asked brightly.

"Trying to concentrate on schoolwork, but it isn't going very well," she confessed sighing.

"Talked to Adam lately?"

"Some," she replied vaguely.

"Do you have time to meet tonight?" Michael asked. "I know it's a long way, but I thought a change of scene might do us both good."

"I can't meet tonight," she answered, "but I would have really liked to."

"That's okay," he replied. "I just thought I'd ask."

"So are you and Anna a couple?" Kelsey asked suddenly.

"Uh, no…why?" Michael responded.

"She seems like a nice kid," she answered, "I was just curious."

"She isn't really a kid, Kels," he told her, "She's only two years younger than us."

"She seems pretty sheltered," Kelsey observed with a strange tone to her voice.

Michael was surprised, but it almost sounded as if Kelsey were a bit jealous.

"Well, if by sheltered, you mean that she's strong in her faith," he said, "that she is. But did you know she's a Senior at the public high school?"

"Interesting," Kelsey said flatly.

"Have you two been chatting at night?" Michael asked, suddenly putting it together.

"Some," she responded vaguely.

"She isn't judging you, Kelsey," Michael reminded her, "she wants you to keep in mind that that's a baby in there."

Kelsey was silent.

"It's pretty easy for someone to say so, when it isn't their life that's falling apart," she said hotly.

"What can we do for you?" Michael asked her, running his fingers through his hair and stretching out in his desk chair. "You just tell me what we can do — how we can help you keep it together and we'll do it for you."

"Tell my parents then," Kelsey shot back at him.

"I'll go with you, if you think that will help," he offered, closing his eyes.

She remained silent.

"Have you told anyone yet, Kelsey?" he asked.

"Yeah, my roommate," she replied.

Michael opened his eyes slowly and waited, looking

absently at his computer screen.

"She said she would go with me to 'take care of it'... Adam said he'd go too."

Michael took a deep breath and clenched his free hand into a fist which he tapped against his thigh angrily. This was exactly the scenario that he didn't want to unfold. Everyone who had access to time with Kelsey was pressuring her to get an abortion.

"What do you think Kelsey? How do you feel?" he pressed.

"I don't know!" she exclaimed, "Wouldn't it be so much easier to just get it done?"

"When you say easier, what do you mean exactly? Do you mean, so you don't have to deal with this right now, or do you mean easier in the long run when you wake up everyday thinking about what you did?"

Kelsey was silent. Michael knew she was angry at him. He also knew that if he had supported her in getting the abortion, it would have been done already. He felt a bit overwhelmed; what if he said the wrong thing? Michael tried to shake those thoughts out of his head. He knew the nature of second guessing and it didn't come from the peace of God.

"I don't know what to do, Michael," Kelsey told him mournfully.

"You are doing everything you need to do right now, Kelsey," he encouraged her. "When you are ready to commit to having this baby and get away from these people, I have plenty of places that you can go."

"Places they won't think I'm crazy?" she asked. He could tell she had started crying.

"Doing the right thing doesn't make you crazy," he told her, "unpopular maybe, but not crazy! I'll come and get you right now if you are ready to go."

She laughed through her tears. "Why does everyone care so much, what I do anyway?"

"I'm sure they just think they are looking out for your best interest," he said gently, "Don't be too upset with them."

"My parents are going to freak," she said finally. He heard muffling sounds on the phone and then Kelsey blowing her nose.

"Yeah, they will," he agreed when the background noise stopped, "and then they will get over it."

"I don't know," she said.

"They can't stop you," he reminded her. "You are over eighteen so they truly have no say."

"I don't want them to hate me," she confessed quietly.

"Kelsey, they will never hate you," Michael told her leaning forward in his seat, "like your friends, they may think that they want the easy option for you. But the easy option isn't the one that's easiest in the end. We'll need to make them see that."

Kelsey sighed. "Isn't it enough to just be pregnant? Do I have to worry about everyone else too?"

"You just worry about you and you let us worry about everyone else," Michael told her. "Look, it's already Wednesday night. What if I plan to meet you on Friday? You can come up here and spend the weekend at Hope and Jessica's place. What time are you done with classes?"

"I'm out at two on Fridays," she replied.

"Do you want to drive all this way or do you want me to meet you?" he asked.

"I think I should drive because then I won't have to tell anyone where I'm going. Everyone here will think I'm at home and everyone at home will think I'm here."

"Alright, then let's plan to have dinner here at my apartment. You can leave your car here and I can bring you to

Hope and Jessica's," he told her, rubbing his leg with his open palm.

"Can't I just stay with you?" she asked petulantly.

"No, sorry," Michael told her, "as much as it might be easier for you to just stay here, now is not the time to get involved in that kind of murky mess. That's a disaster just waiting to happen."

"What does that mean?" Kelsey asked.

"Look Kelsey, I'm no knight in shining armor," he told her, "You are a dear friend of mine in a serious amount of mental and physical trouble. I will not put you in any position that will encourage you to think about me in any way than just a friend. You are the most vulnerable you will ever be in your entire life right now. Falling into another relationship would be the absolute worst thing that could possibly happen to you."

Kelsey was silent.

"It's better this way," he stressed, "I'm sure of it."

"Yeah, alright. Fine," she replied dismissively. "I'll see you for dinner then, on Friday."

"Talk to you tomorrow," he reminded her.

"Yeah, tomorrow."

The phone line went dead. Michael clicked it shut and let out a long sigh. A phone conversation with Kelsey was like running the gauntlet — one moment she seemed open to truth and the next she was the darkest of despair. He knew that until she made her decision most of the rest of their conversations would follow this same pattern.

Wandering out to the kitchen, Michael thought about Kelsey's situation. What a scary place to be. How much he wished that he could have saved her from the pain and difficulties of this life. Once here however, there was no turning back — there would never be a time again when Kelsey was not a mother. Michael stuck his head into the fridge and poked around looking for something to eat. His cell phone, which was lying on the counter vibrated loudly.

"Hey Anna," Michael said, answering it immediately. He wondered if she could hear the smile in his voice as he shut the fridge door.

"Hey there Michael," Anna said softly. "I wanted to call to see how you were and also to see how you thought things were going with Kelsey."

"It's funny you should ask," he remarked, turning around and leaning against the kitchen counter. "I just hung up with Kels a few moments ago."

"How is she doing really?" Anna asked.

"Have you made any headway with her?"

"No, not really. She does call though — faithfully — every night," she responded.

"She knows she needs some good friends, she is just too proud to say so." Michael rubbed his chin, his five o'clock shadow darkening his face.

"We've talked some about Adam," Anna told him.

"Really? What's he like?" Michael was curious. He eased up from the counter and wandered out to the living room. He sat cross-legged on the sofa.

"I'm not sure really... I have a hard time determining if Kelsey is telling me the truth or not," Anna told him.

"She never was much good at lying," he observed.

"Well, if what she is telling me is the truth, Adam sounds like a pretty nice guy who is terrified that his life is going to fall apart around him. Kelsey told me that if his parents were ever to find out, they would demand that Adam and Kelsey get married."

"Really?" Michael was intrigued. "That wasn't the impression that I got about him at all."

"Kelsey said that Adam really believes his parents would

insist because it's 'the right thing to do,'" Anna explained.

"All that Kelsey has said to me is that she's told both Adam and her roommate, both of whom have offered to go with her to the abortion mill."

"She told me that too," Anna said.

There was a pause in the conversation. Michael had his eyes closed and was leaning his head down to his chest.

"Do you think she'll end up going?" Michael asked her finally, opening his eyes and looking up at the crucifix beside the front door of his apartment.

"My gut tells me that she won't," Anna replied. "Of course, I've been praying and hoping as well that she won't. She likes you, you know..."

Michael sighed heavily.

"She's afraid and she feels like she needs me."

"Well, it's true," Anna told him, "She is miserable and you are a bit of sanity for her in this crazy situation."

"I've been very frank with her," Michael protested.

"I know you have," she said gently, "I just wanted to make sure that it was on your radar."

"You are a good person, Anna," Michael told her, letting out a big breath.

She laughed.

"So how is everything else with you?" Michael asked, changing the subject quickly. Sometimes he just wanted to get this whole crazy thing out of his head. It seemed to be enveloping his entire life.

"Oh fine," she replied, "I just finished my last first quarter."

He could tell that she was smiling. "Congratulations!"

"There's going to be a winter formal at school this year," she told him.

"Really?"

"Yeah, it's going to be a holiday fundraiser to raise

money for Toys for Tots. The freshman class is putting it on," she explained.

"That's actually pretty cool," he told her.

After pausing for a moment, he asked, "Are you going to go?"

"I dunno."

"Really? Why not?" he asked, uncrossing his legs and leaning forward putting his elbows on his knees.

"All the people at my school act so stupid when stuff like that comes up. Talk about drama — it's just craziness," she replied seriously.

He laughed. "Do you have to have a date?"

"Well... no," she told him. Her tone expressed this might be an awkward place for the conversation to go.

"Would you like to bring a date?" he pressed.

Anna fidgeted on the other end of the phone.

"Well, yeah, kind of," she confessed honestly, her voice a hoarse whisper. "Everyone there thinks I'm so strange. I mean really, I don't actually care, but ..."

"What do your parents think of the whole thing?" he asked.

"There's another thing…" she said sighing. "This year is prom as well. I don't know if it's worth getting into it twice. It's really just a stupid dance."

A stupid dance that you would like to go to, he thought.

"Did you date in high school?" Anna asked suddenly.

"Actually, I didn't," he told her. "I had lots of friends— guys and girls — and we used to go places together... movies, ice cream, bowling... but I never got involved in the whole dating thing. Way too much drama."

She laughed again.

"About that, I totally agree!" she exclaimed.

They laughed together.

"Any way, I've gotta go. Sorry to talk your ear off," she apologized quietly.

Michael was concerned she might now be embarrassed for confiding in him.

"It was so great to hear from you," he said, "Thank you for being such a great friend, both to me and to Kelsey — even if she doesn't appreciate it much right now."

"It's nothing, really," Anna told him.

"That's not true, Anna. You are such a great person! I'll look forward to talking to you again soon."

"Yeah, okay," she agreed. It sounded as if she was smiling again. "Bye Michael. Have a great week."

Michael clicked the phone shut and tossed it onto the sofa. Anna was such a pleasant person in such a difficult position, being a strong Catholic in a public school. He knew that she spoke out at school, willing to share her convictions with her friends and classmates. He admired her strength. Back when he was in high school, even though it was not all that long ago, the world was much less politically correct than it had become.

Michael grabbed his phone suddenly and flicked it phone open. He was just about to call Timothy Warner's number and ask him if he could escort Anna to the dance when he suddenly froze. It had just occurred to him that Anna might not want to go with him to the dance. Perhaps she would consider him goofy and an embarrassment in front of her friends. The problem was, she was too kind to ever say so. If he wrangled a positive response from Mr. Warner — he would feel even worse about it if she went because she felt obligated.

Michael clicked the phone shut again, shaking his head and running his hand through his hair. How many more complications could he take?

He headed back into the kitchen to get some dinner for real this time. How he ended up in the middle of these things he did not know. This time at least, he had stopped himself before he made a mess of everything. Anna's friendship was important - too important to mess around with.

The front door opened and Michael's roommate, Dave, came in.

"Hey, didn't expect to see you here," Dave called to Michael as he shrugged out of his coat.

"Want dinner?" Michael asked, putting a pot of water on the stove, "Its spaghetti."

"No, but thanks... I'm meeting Jenna for a bite and then early movie. They are running a $5 night over in Liberty Heights," Dave explained.

"Hey, that's cool," Michael responded.

Dave headed down the hall to his room. "Justin should be home though," he called over his shoulder, "he didn't mention having any plans."

Michael did not respond; he was already eating a piece of bread and butter.

Five minutes later, the door opened again. Michael was pouring the spaghetti into the boiling water as Justin came in.

"Hey man. There's enough for you too," Michael told him.

"Great," Justin said, "bachelor food."

"Yeah well, poor college student food is more like," Michael retorted.

Justin laughed. "It could be Ramen. I'll be right back."

Michael stirred the spaghetti quickly. When the timer beeped, he drained it in the kitchen sink and then added some canned sauced to the warm pot. Pouring the spaghetti back in, he mixed it quickly. He divided the cooked spaghetti onto two plates and put a piece of Italian bread on each one. He put the plates on the table and got glasses and milk from the kitchen.

Justin hustled back to the table as Michael was pulling in his seat.

"This is a nice treat," he said.

"Yeah well, that's because you haven't eaten it yet," Michael joked.

"Who messes up spaghetti?" Justin asked, digging in.

The two of them ate hungrily as Dave got ready to go out.

"Kisses to Jenna," Justin teased as Dave walked to the closet to grab his coat.

"She loves you too," Dave replied laughing, "I won't be late. See you guys later."

"Bye." Michael and Justin spoke in unison.

"So how are things going with you?" Justin asked, mopping up sauce with his piece of Italian bread.

"Everything is fine," Michael replied.

"And how are things with your friend Kelsey?" Justin regarded Michael steadily.

Michael did not respond at first.

"Are you two in some kind of trouble?"

Michael shook his head.

"No, it's not like that," he responded, "Kelsey is truly just a friend of mine from high school. She's in a bit of a bind, but it has nothing to do with me."

Justin nodded his head. "I would have been surprised, but I still felt I should ask."

Michael nodded. "I understand."

"So what's going to happen with all that?" Justin wondered.

"Don't know yet," Michael replied, putting his fork down on his empty plate. "You all done?"

Justin handed Michael his empty plate.

"Leave them on the counter if you have homework. I can do them."

"Thanks Justin," Michael said, stacking the plates, cups and utensils and carrying them into the kitchen. He put them on the counter next to the sink and turning, headed into his room.

Michael spent some time after dinner lying on his bed and catching up on his reading for Catechism. Finally, he shut the book and put it aside. He stood up and stretched. He walked over to his desk and leaning down, he pulled the laptop over. He had stopped writing in the middle of a paragraph which was unlike him. Kelsey's story was weighing heavily on his heart so he sank into the chair and dove right into a completely new section of his manuscript. His writing had been dwindling to a slow crawl since the semester had begun. Now he felt a renewed sense to get working on it.

As he typed steadily, a reminder suddenly popped up on his screen. Michael had forgotten that he had agreed to give a talk to a local youth group this Friday night. He frowned realizing the predicament this was going to put him in. His dinner plans with Kelsey would need to be put on hold – or he could ask her to come along. He grimaced at the thought. Of course, he could check in with Jessica and Hope to see what their plans were or connect with Anna to see if she was available. Besides all of those details, Michael would need to spend some time writing his talk.

Losing traction on the story, he flipped open his phone quickly and called his friend Kevin.

"Hey Kevin," Michael said to voicemail. "I just wanted to call to confirm with you for Friday night. I've got 7 pm on my calendar and I also wanted to know where you were at in terms of topics to discuss… Thanks."

Michael considered calling Kelsey, but thought better of it. He wanted to have a more concrete plan to offer her before connecting with her again. He knew that it would be precarious for her to consider doing something other than hanging out with him for the evening. He had better hold off on telling her about it until he could find something to sweeten the deal.

Anna's phone rang at precisely nine o'clock that night. She knew it would be Kelsey before she even answered it. She quickly made the sign of the cross, while moving to her desk to grab the cell phone.

"Hello Kelsey," Anna said pleasantly, "how was your day?"

"Hi," Kelsey said flatly. She cringed as she said it. She had no idea why she felt the need to continually be cross with Anna — it's not like the poor girl had done anything but try to be her friend. She stood up from her desk chair and launched out of her small dorm room.

"It's good to hear from you," Anna tried again.

Kelsey didn't respond for a moment. She was breathing quickly as if she were walking.

"Do you know Michael's friends, Jessica and Hope?" Kelsey asked curiously.

"Yeah, I do. They're wonderful!" Anna replied.

Kelsey cringed again.

"Michael wants me to go and stay at Jessica's for the weekend," Kelsey told her, a note of complaint in her voice.

"I think you'll really like Jessica," Anna offered, "She's a lot of fun to be around."

"I don't understand why we can't just stay at Michael's," Kelsey said, baiting her.

Anna thought a moment before responding.

"That probably isn't a great idea," was all she responded.

"I don't see why," Kelsey snapped, pushing out of the front door of her dorm and stopping on the sidewalk. "Why?

Would it bother you? Do you and Michael have something going on?"

"No, Michael is just a friend of mine," Anna replied. She sank onto her bed and tried not to sigh out loud. This wasn't the first time they had strayed into this topic of conversation.

"Well, what if Michael asked you out?" Kelsey pressed, a cool evening breeze wiping her black hair into her face. She pushed it aside angrily. "Are you interested?"

Anna took a deep breath and then answered quickly. "It wouldn't really matter; I'm not allowed to date."

Kelsey laughed caustically on the other end of the phone and resumed her brisk walk. "You aren't allowed to date?" she asked with disdain.

"My father doesn't believe there's any reason for me to be alone with a boy," Anna explained honestly.

"How old are you?"

"I'm eighteen."

"Do you always do what your father says?" Kelsey asked sarcastically.

"I do if I want to stay living in his house," Anna told her. She could just imagine Kelsey rolling her eyes and shaking her head on the other end of the phone.

"Is he going to let you out of his sight to go to college?" Kelsey asked, still sarcastic, letting out a long breath. She had crossed the quad and was standing alone beneath a street light. Not many folks were out on campus at this time of night and she suddenly felt completely isolated from those few she saw walking in one direction or another.

Anna didn't respond to Kelsey's jibe. She had no intention of getting into an argument with Kelsey. Anna knew that she was bearing the brunt of Kelsey's anger.

"I'm sorry," Kelsey mumbled, looking over at the window of her dorm room from across the quad. In her haste to leave, she had left on all the lights. "I guess that wasn't very nice."

"You're right," Anna retorted, still honest. And before Kelsey could respond, she added, "but that's okay. I forgive you."

Kelsey sighed, rolling her eyes and beginning to walk in the direction of her dorm. Anna and Michael sounded just alike, always making references to their religion.

"Honestly Anna," she said after a moment. "I don't know why I'm always such a bitch."

"It's not that big a deal," Anna said. "I don't take it personally."

"So you think Jessica and Hope are pretty cool?" Kelsey asked, trying to take the conversation to a more civilized place. She couldn't understand why Anna kept bothering with her every night. If it were Kelsey, she would just have let the call go to voicemail.

"Yeah, they're both a lot of fun," Anna replied. "They do all sorts of cool stuff. They aren't like your usual adults."

Kelsey actually laughed in response.

"Well, that's good, I've had enough of clueless adults to deal with lately."

"Does that mean you've told your parents?" Anna asked.

"No," Kelsey snapped.

There was an awkward pause.

"Michael said he would go with me to tell them," Kelsey said, back to her baiting tone of voice.

"Yeah, that sounds like something Michael would do," Anna responded. "He really is a great guy."

"How long have you known each other?" Kelsey asked.

"I dunno, a couple of years at least," Anna said.

"How long have you liked him?" Kelsey asked again.

Forever, Anna thought, *but he just sees in me some little kid.*

To Kelsey, she replied, "Like I said before — it really doesn't matter whether I like him or not. Nothing can come of it — not for years anyway."

Kelsey frowned. She knew that Anna was being purposefully vague with her and it bothered her.

"Why can't you just be straight with me?" she pressed.

"Look Kelsey, I've got school to finish. I'm glad you're doing okay," Anna told her, knowing the conversation would be going nowhere good from here. "I've really gotta go."

"Yeah, whatever," Kelsey replied.

"Talk to you tomorrow?" Anna asked.

"I suppose."

"Try and get some rest," Anna suggested.

Kelsey frowned as she pulled open the door to her dorm. Like she needed to take advice from a girl who wasn't even allowed to date!

"Whatever," Kelsey replied.

"Good night, Kelsey," Anna told her.

"Yeah, bye."

Anna listened to the phone click off from Kelsey's end and she tossed her cell phone to the side of her bed. There was a soft knock on the door. Anna knew it would be her mom to check in and see how the phone call went.

"Come in," Anna said quietly, leaning back into her pillows and closing her eyes.

Lily opened the door just wide enough to enter. She walked over to Anna's bed and sat on the edge.

Anna leaned up straight and looked at her mother. Her eyes filled with tears of frustration.

"We already know Kelsey is difficult," Lily reminded her daughter, leaning over to tuck a stray strand of Anna's dark wavy hair behind her ear.

"She frustrates me so much!" Anna exclaimed, taking a

deep breath. "All she wants to discuss is whether or not Michael and I are a couple."

Lily chuckled softly.

"I don't know why she keeps calling me, Mom," Anna confessed. "The girl thinks I'm a freak."

Anna grinned lopsidedly.

Lily patted her on the leg as Anna's moment of frustration passed.

"It doesn't matter what she thinks," Lily reminded her gently, "It's what she sees in you that keeps her calling back."

Anna nodded her head.

"Let's pray for Kelsey, just the two of us," Lily suggested bowing her head.

Anna bowed her head as well and listened to her mother speak soft words of tender compassion on Kelsey's behalf. A wave of thankfulness broke over Anna as she peered up and watched her mother praying earnestly for a girl either of them barely knew.

A state away, Kelsey lay face down on her bed in her empty dorm room, sobbing into her pillow.

CHAPTER SIX
The Message

 ichael woke on Friday morning somewhat agitated. He heard from Kevin the night before and had put off calling Kelsey to tell her about the change in plans. He figured he would just wait for her Friday

call in to tell her about his previously scheduled activity. Michael was also upset because Kevin had explained that some of his teens had heard about the ruckus at St. Monica's and he was hoping Michael could answer some questions  about communion between faiths. He wanted to make some extra time to review his Catechism.

Michael was just getting out of the shower when he heard his cell phone ring in the other room. Pulling a towel tightly around him, he padded barefoot on the cold floor down the hall to his bedroom. This trek from the warm bathroom into the cold morning did nothing to improve his mood.

"Hi Kelsey," he said into the phone.

"Hi yourself," she said back.

"It's good to hear from you this lovely morning," he said, heading back into the warm bathroom.

"We still on for tonight?" she asked.

"Slight change of plan," he told her, leaning back against the bathroom sink. "I forgot that I need to speak to my friend Kevin's youth group over in East Longmeadow at 7 p.m. We can still eat as long as you get here early enough and then you can just go with me to the Youth Group before we head over to Jessica's."

There was silence on the other end.

"Come on, Kels, give me a break," Michael pleaded, "I'm sorry but I forgot all about it."

"Any excuse to ply me with religion, is that it Michael?"

"Don't be ridiculous," he told her, cradling the phone with his shoulder and beginning to dry his feet with a fluffy brown towel. "You don't have to come with me. I can invite Anna to join us for dinner or Jessica can come and get you. In fact, you can probably drive straight over there if you want to, but she's all the way in Stafford Springs."

"Sounds like fun," she said sarcastically, "isn't that all the way in Connecticut?"

"What do you want me to say to you, Kelsey?" he asked, "I've already apologized."

"Yeah, okay — fine, whatever," she replied.

"Does that mean you're going to come with me or what?" he asked, pulling on his robe.

"Fine, yeah, I'll go with you," she said.

"Great! It'll be fun, you'll see."

"Fun — yeah, whatever," she said dubiously.

"I'll see you tonight then," he said. "Meet me here at the apartment."

"Alright, bye," she answered.

Michael hung up and headed to his room to find

something to wear. He grabbed a pair of clean jeans and a worn navy tee-shirt with a white logo that had half peeled off. It was for some Park and Rec baseball team he had helped coach a few summers ago.

There were no classes on Fridays at Our Lady of Guadalupe because the seminarians who were the largest majority went out on fieldwork that day. But the library would still be open and he wanted to go for a few hours to see if he could finally get caught up with his schoolwork.

His phone rang again and this time it was Jessica laughing on the other end.

"Are you awake?" she asked.

He laughed with her. "Yeah."

"Well I know you don't have classes on Friday so I thought I might wake you up," she explained still laughing.

"What's funny?" Michael asked, grabbing his book bag and walking down the short hall.

"I was just reading this funny email when you picked up. I figured I would get your machine so I was multi-tasking, thought I would just leave a message."

"I've already showered and talked to Kelsey this morning," he announced proudly, grabbing an apple out of the basket on the kitchen counter.

"That's good for you for ten o'clock," she remarked, "I just wanted to double check about Kelsey — she still coming to stay for the weekend?"

"Unless she blows me off, she should be here," he answered, taking a large bite out of the apple. "She said she would go with me to youth group in Long Meadow before I take her over to your place." He finished speaking with the apple bite held between his teeth.

"Nice manners," Jessica remarked. "It's lucky I can understand 'boy.'"

Michael responded by chewing loudly in her ear. As he grinned, he imagined her shaking her head on the other end of the phone.

"I have no idea what I'm going to talk about," he told her once he swallowed the apple. "Kevin wants me to answer questions about the communion debate at St. Monica's."

"What did the Warners decide? Are they going to leave St. Monica's?," Jessica asked.

"Dunno."

"Well, what do you think? If you were in that parish, would you get out?" she pressed.

"Oh totally. For me, it's very cut and dry. But then I'm not the principal of the High School right next door. So anyhow, pray for my talk because you know how teens are... They ask twenty-five stupid questions because they are afraid of asking the one question that really matters. I hope I'll get a couple live ones."

"Okay, I'll say the Mercy Chaplet when you're speaking.... So I'll see you later tonight then with Kelsey?"

"Yeah but probably not until sometime after nine," he answered.

"No problem; come whenever," she told him.

"See ya then."

Michael finished eating the apple in a couple of quick bites. He went back to his room to look for one more library book due today, which he found peeking out from beneath the corner of his bed. He shoved it into his open book bag and then, sliding the laptop bag over his shoulder, he grabbed his coat and headed out the door.

<hr />

Fridays were always quiet on campus. This semester, some of the lay students had signed up for work period, so they could help out around the place. Michael parked in the half-full commuter lot on the side closest to the library. He ran into a handful of students who were busy cleaning up the areas outside of the library building. He waved to them, knowing each one personally.

He entered the library and greeted the Brother at the circulation desk. He went directly into the back room to find an empty computer station and got himself set up. He knew he had better pay some attention to his schoolwork before he got too far off track taking care of Kelsey. He wouldn't be able to later, if things reached crisis proportions.

After about two hours of focused schoolwork, Michael felt his stomach grumbling and realized it was already past twelve o'clock. He decided to get over to the refectory before they stopped serving lunch. Leaving his things setup in the library, he walked over to the dining area empty handed.

Michael got his food quickly and silently. Fridays were silent days for all seminarians who weren't out on field study. He went into the staff room to eat because sitting with his friends would be too much of a temptation to talk. Fr. Sullivan, the rector, came ambling in with his food tray just as Michael finished praying. He watched Michael sit alone and he came in that direction.

"May I join you?" Fr. Sullivan asked.

Michael motioned with his hand since he was busy chewing with his mouth. He flushed just a little at being caught in such dingy clothes with his mouth full of food.

"Hello Father," Michael said, once the priest had given thanks and joined him at the table. After rubbing his hand quickly on the leg of his jeans, he offered the rector his hand.

"How are things going with you, my friend?" Fr. Sullivan asked kindly, shaking Michael's outstretched hand.

"I'm worried about the Warners," Michael replied honestly, pulling in his seat.

Fr. Sullivan nodded his head. "Difficult situation."

"Father, do you think they should leave St. Monica's?" Michael asked abruptly.

"I am concerned what the message will be if they stay, but Tim also must be concerned with the welfare of his family and his financial security," Father replied.

"Yeah, but suppose he's the Eucharistic minister and he knows the person presenting himself for communion isn't Catholic?" Michael asked, "I have heard that a priest shouldn't refuse Communion to anyone unless he is absolutely sure that it will be scandalous. When I served as a Eucharistic minister over the summer for our parish camp weekend, my Pastor told me that if I had direct knowledge that someone was living in sin, I should offer them a blessing first and only give them communion when they asked."

"Did you do that?" Fr. Sullivan inquired.

Michael nodded.

"And did anyone ever ask?"

Shaking his head, Michael replied, "Nope."

"I believe that Tim should certainly step aside from any active ministry in his parish until this issue is resolved," Father told him, "even if he doesn't leave the parish altogether."

Michael nodded thoughtfully.

Fr. Sullivan asked about Michael's ministry work and the two talked for a short time. As soon as he had finished eating, Michael thanked the rector for his time and cleared both sets of lunch dishes. After depositing the trays in the kitchen, he glanced at his watch. He had been speaking with Fr. Sullivan for over an hour: so much for a quick bite to eat. He headed back over to the library where he spent the rest of the afternoon diligently paying attention to his schoolwork.

On his way off campus a few hours later, Michael decided to stop over at the adoration chapel to pray. The small chapel was empty except for one older man who was praying a Rosary. Michael saw him fingering the beads and moving his lips though he made no sound.

Kneeling in the back of the chapel and closing his eyes, Michael did not realize how upset he was about the Warners until this moment in the quiet chapel. So many scenarios were running through his head. He prayed fervently for his friends. He prayed also that God would give him the right words to share with the kids at youth group tonight. He hoped to speak the truth and tell them that this circumstance was a man-made affair, and not something that had come from Rome — in point of fact, it had not even been approved by Rome which was just another indication that it was not the right plan for any parish at this time. Michael meditated silently for a long while, thinking about how he would feel if he were pushed into the same situation as the Warners. He had always looked up to Timothy and he realized suddenly that in a few years' time, he could honestly be facing the same kind of circumstance in his own life. He prayed for strength — for himself and also for Timothy.

The door to the chapel opened quietly. Glancing over, Michael saw one of the professors from the school come in. At the same time, the older gentleman finished up his Rosary and got to his feet slowly. The gentleman and the professor exchanged a knowing glance as the older man passed by — so much to pray for, so little time.

Michael's thoughts drifted to Kelsey and he began to pray for her earnestly as he continued to kneel in the back of the chapel. Suddenly, the words from his conversation with his father came back to mind and he made a decision to talk to Kelsey tonight about whether or not she knew of any other girls in her school that were also pregnant. After spending a few more minutes in the quiet chapel, Michael made the sign of the cross slowly, got to his feet and made his way to the door.

Arriving home, Michael was able to put his talk for the youth group together in a relatively short amount of time. He knew it was because he had stopped at the chapel — his head was a bit clearer now and he was much less agitated than he had been this morning. He had some time before Kelsey was due at the apartment so he went into the kitchen to decide on something for dinner. Neither of his roommates would be back for the weekend — they were traveling to upstate New York for a family wedding. Sometimes having room mates who were brothers paid off.

Michael decided on pancakes — they would be cheap, easy and fun. He wandered back into the living room and clicked on the television. He should probably be working on more schoolwork, but he was spent. He needed to spend some time just doing something mindless.

A loud knock on the door woke Michael from a sound sleep. He sat up groggily. The sun had set and he only had the light from the television on. The knocking came again, more impatiently this time and his cell phone began to ring from his bedroom. He hurried over and opened the door.

"I was freaking out!" Kelsey pushed past him with a large duffle bag and a frown on her face. "I thought that you had gone out for some reason and there was no one home."

Michael watched her breeze in.

Kelsey tossed her duffle onto the floor next to the sofa and turned to face him. She put her hands on her hips and swung her black hair angrily.

Michael walked over and shut the door behind her.

"Sorry, I guess I fell asleep."

Kelsey glared at him and sank down onto the sofa, curling her feet up under her. She had on her jeans with the rip in the knee, a bright red tank and her overly large black hoodie.

Michael clicked on some lights.

"You look tired," he told her.

"I didn't get a mid-afternoon nap," she retorted.

"It's good to see you Kelsey," he said instead of taking her bait, "how are you feeling?"

She looked at him steadily as he sat cross-legged on the floor. "I don't feel any different."

"How far along are you exactly?" he asked, yawning.

"Two months or so," she replied. "Shouldn't I be sick by now or something?" She played with her ring and avoided looking at Michael.

"Everyone handles it differently," he told her.

She nodded her head. "I am feeling really tired though."

"Listen, I have a question for you," Michael said, "do you know of any other girls out your way who might be expecting also?"

She looked straight over at him, confused.

"What are you, starting a crusade or something?" she asked, "isn't just one enough for you?"

"One is plenty enough," he responded, "I was just wondering that's all."

"Why?"

"Well, I talked to my Dad…"

"You told your Dad?!" Kelsey jumped to her feet. "What are you, stupid?!"

She began to pace in front of the fireplace.

"Kelsey, relax," he told her. "My father was talking about some issues he's been researching… anyway, he said that in the past few months, pregnancy among teen girls is on the rise and for some reason, it seems to be happening in clusters."

"What does that mean?" she asked, sitting back down on the couch. "And what's it have to do with me?"

"I'm not sure exactly," Michael replied, "but I figured

I would ask you and see if there are other girls from your school that are also expecting. There seems to be some kind of scientific trend."

Kelsey thought for a few moments.

"I don't know anyone," she confessed, "but it isn't like everyone is really talking about it."

Michael nodded.

"What's for dinner anyway?" she asked changing the subject.

"Pancakes."

"Pancakes? Cool," she replied.

She followed Michael into the kitchen. He grabbed a box of pancake mix from the cupboard, a large plastic bowl and a wire whisk.

"Milk and eggs from the fridge," he directed Kelsey.

She got him the rest of the ingredients from the refrigerator and then took a seat at the small table, watching him measuring and mixing.

"Can you get plates and things?" he asked, pointing to another cabinet and a drawer near the stove.

Kelsey got up wearily and got out two plates, forks and mugs.

Once they were sitting at the table with a plate of steaming pancakes in front of them, Kelsey asked, "Okay, so what's going on tonight anyway?"

"Can we pray first?" Michael asked her.

"You pray, I'll watch."

"You know this one, Kels — the words haven't changed."

She frowned but then laughed and blessed herself when he did.

"As I was saying," she began when he was finished.

"So tonight, we're going to talk at my friend, Kevin's, youth group in East Longmeadow," he interrupted her, stabbing a stack of three pancakes from the steaming plate.

"I don't think WE are going to talk about anything," she retorted, "You may have some very interesting things to say, but you are on your own."

Michael laughed. "Oh come on, you're a natural."

"Yeah, whatever," she said clearly not amused, "I'm not talking in front of a group of kids about anything."

"Alright, fine. Make me do all the hard stuff by myself." He was teasing her. "And after that, we'll drive out to Jessica's. Maybe we should rent a movie on our way over there or something…"

"I don't know," she replied uncertainly, her fork hesitating in mid-air.

"Well, movie or not, that's the plan," he told her.

Kelsey and Michael talked easily as they ate. When they had finished, she helped him clean up in the kitchen. He washed, she dried and he put everything away.

"What time are we supposed to be there?" Kelsey asked, wiping her hands on a dishtowel.

"In about an hour," he told her.

"Mind if I lie down for a little while?" she asked.

He shook his head. "I need to review my talk anyway. I'll get you up in about forty minutes."

She turned and stepped into the living room but stopped short. "Where?"

"You can use my room. It's the one on the right."

She walked down the hall and headed over to Michael's room to rest.

Forty minutes later, Michael was shaking Kelsey lightly. She had fallen completely asleep.

"Do you want to stay here and rest? I can come and get you later," he asked her quietly.

"No, I'll come with you," she replied groggily.

She got out of the bed and went down the hall to the bathroom.

Michael walked in the opposite direction and gathered their coats and Kelsey's duffle. She came out of the bathroom, rubbing the sleep from her eyes. He helped her into her jacket and led her out of the apartment.

"I had the strangest dream," she confided to him as they made their way to the car.

"Do you want to tell me about it?" he asked.

She was silent for a few minutes. She waited until he had gone around and gotten into the car beside her.

"Yeah, I dreamed that I was holding a little baby girl," she said softly.

He did not respond. He did not start the car. He just sat quietly looking over at Kelsey.

"Michael, I think that I know what I need to do now," she told him.

His eyes immediately filled with tears and he pulled Kelsey into a fierce hug.

"I'm still really afraid," she told him, crying into his chest.

"It's okay to be afraid," he told her, crying himself. "You have plenty of people who will help you, Kelsey. You just have to be willing to let them."

"I know," she said, pushing him away from her and digging in her hoodie pocket for a tissue. "I've really been a bitch to your friends, haven't I?"

"No one is judging you, Kelsey. Not because of your situation and certainly not because of the way you've been acting. My friends all realize the gravity of this situation. Do you think any of them haven't wondered how they would have handled the same if they were in your shoes right now?"

"Yes, but they have been nothing but nice to me," she protested, dabbing her eyes with a tissue.

"Well, there's ample time to apologize if you feel that's necessary," he reminded her.

They sat in silence for a moment. Michael looked down and said a quick prayer of Thanksgiving.

"Are you ready to head out?" he asked, putting his hand on the steering wheel.

She nodded her head.

The drive to the church in Long Meadow was quick; Michael stayed off the highway and took only back roads to get there. They were about five minutes late.

Michael was apologizing to Kevin as they walked into a hall full of teens that were talking loudly and amusing one another with the ringtones on their cell phones. A group of adults stood to the side, talking quietly among themselves.

Kevin called the room to attention and began the evening with a prayer. The kids stood reluctantly and mumbled along.

Kelsey took a seat in the back and watched as Michael began to interact with the teens. He truly had a gift. In a few moments, he had them laughing together as he crossed the room standing on his hands. Farther into his talk, he even moved some of the girls to tears as he talked about the situation with his sister Sarah. Kelsey shifted uncomfortably as Michael told another story of a friend he knew who had recently gotten pregnant.

No one noticed her sitting, way in the back, but she felt like a bright spotlight was shining down on her. She shaded her eyes with her hand and looked down to the floor. After a moment of silence, she looked up and into Michael's eyes. He looked at her pleadingly. He was trying to will her to stand up and share with this group. She held his gaze for a moment and then shook her head imperceptibly.

A moment later she was moved to tears as the room burst into spontaneous applause. He finished the story by letting them know that the mom would have the baby.

An hour had already flown by so Michael opened the floor for questions. Immediately, one young girl raised her hand.

"Can you please explain to me why the pastor at St. Monica's said he would give Holy Communion to anyone no matter whether they are Catholics or not?"

Michael took a deep breath as he noticed everyone sit up a bit straighter in their seats. No time like the present, he thought, glancing at Kevin who gave him the thumbs up sign.

"Actually, No, I can't tell you why the pastor would suggest such a thing," he said matter-of-factly, grabbing a nearby chair and sitting on it backwards. Resting his hands on the back of the chair and facing the roomful of teens he went on, "I can however, talk to you briefly about the Eucharist and what it is."

The students fidgeted in their seats. Michael looked briefly to Kevin who just nodded.

"I'm sure that many of you know, or at least remember from First Communion year, how the Eucharist becomes the true body, blood, soul and divinity of Jesus Christ."

Low murmuring broke out in the audience.

"You don't have to believe me," Michael told them, "but to be Catholic; you need to believe this part of church teaching. If you don't, you aren't really Catholic…"

He let that settle for a few moments before continuing. "Our Church also teaches that only those Catholics free from grave sin are to present themselves for Communion. What this means is that the responsibility of going to Communion rests more with the person than with the priest. The priest however, is supposed to encourage Catholics who do not live Church teaching in their public lives — pro-abortion politicians, for example — to refrain from presenting themselves for Communion until they are ready to repent."

"Well, how do you know if someone repents, then?" a young guy yelled out from the back.

"You don't know," Michael responded, looking in the direction of the voice. "That is between the person, the priest and God. For that reason, we can't pretend to know who should and shouldn't be presenting themselves for Communion."

"But if the priests are now going to give Communion to just anyone, what difference does it make?" the same young guy asked.

"Just because one man or a few men in the Church decide to do things differently..." Michael paused here to say a quick prayer... "doesn't change the real teaching of the Church. Regardless of who goes to Communion, when the priest says the words of consecration, the bread and wine are transformed into the real Jesus Christ. And anyone who presents himself for Communion should be both a baptized Catholic and free from grave sin."

No one responded for a few moments.

Then the girl who first asked the question raised her hand again. "So what you are saying then is that the Pastor of St. Monica's was wrong?"

"No man has authority to govern the Church of Jesus Christ except for the Vicar of Christ who resides in Rome," Michael answered her.

"Did this decree come from Rome?" the girl pressed.

"What's your name, hon?" Michael asked, standing up and walking in her direction.

"Amanda," she replied quietly.

"No Amanda; the suggestions of the Pastor at St. Monica's came from him only and not from Rome," he told her.

A new wave of fidgeting filled the room. This time however, there was a new sense of urgency that had not been there before.

"So what do we do then?" asked the same guy from the back, "Do we leave St. Monica's? I'm at St. Agnes, but I often go to St. Monica's with my friends from there."

"I'm not an authority on this, but I can tell you that first we should pray," Michael answered immediately. "And then we should take every opportunity to share the faith the way it has been handed down to us through the Vicar of Christ in Rome."

"Well, is the Pope going to do something about it?" Amanda demanded.

"Amanda, I wish I had an answer to that question," Michael said, standing before her. "First it will be addressed by the Bishop here. That comes way before the news goes onto the Pope."

Amanda nodded in understanding.

"The fact is," this he addressed to the room at large, "I'm just some poor college student who was invited here to speak to you by your Youth Minister, Kevin. I am not an authority on this issue and I have no way of knowing what will happen. I do encourage you however, to talk to your priests. Let them know what you have been taught about the truth of the faith."

Another young man raised his hand from the middle of the crowd and Michael motioned for him to speak.

"But do you really think that Jesus would turn people away like we do?" he demanded.

"I believe what I know about Jesus from the Gospels," Michael challenged him. "And when Jesus spoke about being the Bread of Life in John Chapter 6, he never changed what he was saying because most of his followers got up and left. If you don't know the story, I'll just get to the main facts. In John 6:55-56, Jesus says 'For my flesh is food indeed, and my blood is drink indeed. He who eats my flesh and drinks my blood abides in me, and I in him.' Then further along in verse 60, some of the disciples say 'This is a hard saying; who can listen to it?' and they take off. What does Jesus do? He watches them go. It never says in the story that he tries to stop them from going. Instead, Jesus turns to the twelve and asks if they will leave also. Note that he doesn't say to those twelve — 'you know what, I think those folks misunderstood what I said. When I was talking about food and drink I didn't really mean MY body and blood.' He has every chance to tell them that he was misunderstood, but he never does. What he says instead is in verse 65 when he says, 'This is why I told you that no one can come to me unless it is granted him by the Father."

The kids were enraptured by what Michael was telling them. He felt anxious for a moment, like he was carrying a great weight as he walked back and forth slowly, in front of the small crowd. But then he turned back to the same young man saying, "So what do you think? Do you think Jesus means what he says and says what he means?"

The young man looked at Michael quizzically. "It makes sense…what you are saying."

Kevin stood up then and Michael felt a rush of relief run through him. He had survived another round. He noticed Kelsey watching him from the back of the room and he suddenly felt a wave of discomfort. He pushed the feeling away and focused instead on some of the kids who had approached him to ask a few more questions or just shake his hand and say thank you.

By nine o'clock, the crowd had thinned out enough that Michael felt comfortable leaving. Kevin seemed pleased by the way the evening had gone and had even tossed out the idea of Michael returning to speak on some other themes. Michael put him off but agreed to think about it.

Michael and Kelsey drove the first part of the trip to Jessica's in total silence. The only sound was the radio playing quietly in the background. Michael was processing how he felt about the tenor of the evening and Kelsey was lost in thought all on her own.

"You really have a way with teens," Kelsey said finally, "I could never do anything like that."

Michael looked over at her. "It really isn't me at all."

"They respond to you so well."

"It helps that the girls think I'm good looking," he said. "And the boys think that walking on your hands is cool." They both laughed. The ice seemed to be broken again and they conversed more freely.

"You really believe all that you were explaining to the kids?" she asked.

"You mean about the Body and Blood of Christ?" he asked.

She nodded. "It's all so abstract to me."

"All relationships take work, Kelsey," he told her. "Do you really expect your relationship with Christ to be any different?"

She did not respond.

"I bet that if you woke up every morning and said a short prayer to begin your day — in one week's time, you would be looking at things differently."

"You make it seem so effortless," she observed.

Michael laughed. "It's anything but effortless. I promise!"

"You know Michael, sometimes I feel like I'm so lost. I don't even know who I am anymore."

He stayed silent.

"There were so many things that I took for granted, so many things that I believed in… look at my life now. What happened?"

He did not respond immediately.

"How long has it been since you had a real heart to heart with God?" he asked her finally.

She did not respond, but turned instead to look out of

the car window and away from Michael.

"Maybe God has been trying to get your attention again, Kelsey," he offered.

"But did it have to be so earth-shattering?"

"It appears that subtlety was not working with you."

She looked back in his direction, smiled slightly and then she sighed.

"So what do I do now?" she asked him.

"You mean about the baby?" he asked.

She nodded her head.

"Well, if you are two or three months along and this is November, then I would say that you definitely should finish up this semester at school. You will most likely not be showing by finals time. Take next semester off and stay somewhere that you will be well supported."

"Not with my folks then," she murmured.

"Let's cross that bridge when we get there," Michael suggested. "And then you can have the summer to get back on your feet and head back to the school in the fall."

"It sounds so simple," Kelsey said, leaning her head against the cool car window.

"Well, it helps not to make it any more complicated than necessary," he replied.

"And what do you know about adoption?" she asked him quietly.

"That's one subject that I really don't know all that much about. My parents and my sister left me out of those discussions, for the most part. I know that there are some options now — depending on the kind of involvement both you and the adoptive family are comfortable with."

"It just sounds weird to talk about," she said.

"I would guess Kelsey, that this is the hardest thing that you will ever do."

"Are we almost there?" she asked in a small voice after the silence grew for a long while.

Michael knew that the conversation had ended for now. But he was grateful for every step they took closer to a decision based in reality and not in emotion.

CHAPTER SEVEN
Safe Haven

 ichael and Kelsey arrived at Jessica's little ranch-style house shortly after ten. The house was a bustle of activity, even at that late hour. Neither Hope nor Jessica had their children with them for the weekend; the kids were with their Dads. The women did not want to overwhelm Kelsey with motherly attention so they had decided to bake a couple varieties of cookies. Both were in the kitchen: one slim and fair with dark hair and eyes; the other full-figured, a bit shorter with strawberry-blonde hair. They were  both covered in flour, talking and laughing when Michael and Kelsey let themselves in.

"You finally made it," Jessica said, glancing over her shoulder as Michael led Kelsey into the small kitchen.

Michael and Kelsey, along with their bags, took up most of the space near the doorway.

"How did it go?" Hope asked, wiping her hands on a dishtowel and walking out of the kitchen into the entrance to the front room so the two could pass through the small space. She pulled the hair elastic out of her dark brown hair and made the bun tighter before twirling the elastic back around it.

Michael took a few steps forward and held up Kelsey's large bag.

"She'll stay in Stevie's room," Jessica told him, turning her attention to the oven. Her strawberry-blonde hair was also pulled back and Michael could see small beads of perspiration on the back of her neck. "Kelsey can use the trundle bed."

Michael led Kelsey through the cramped, warm kitchen, past Hope who was peeling off Alicia's zip up hoodie while standing in the entrance to the front room. He lugged the bags down the narrow hallway as Kelsey followed farther into the small house. Hope tossed the hoodie onto the couch and returned to the kitchen, as they passed. Kelsey could hear the two women continuing to laugh as if they had never been interrupted.

"What's their story?" Kelsey asked, turning inside the small bedroom and fixing her gaze on Michael. She raised a perfectly shaped black eyebrow.

Michael put her bag down on top of Stephen's small bed. He sighed tiredly and ran a hand through his hair as his blue eyes seemed to lose focus for a moment. She could see he was tired.

"No story really," he told her, looking back up and focusing on her expression. "They are both single moms. They moved next door to one another so they could help each other out."

She continued to gaze at him quizzically.

"They have another friend, Martha, also a single mom, who lives three doors down. It works really well for all of them." Michael turned away from her and headed back down the narrow hallway into the kitchen.

Jessica was just putting another batch of chocolate chip cookies into the oven. Since she was distracted, Michael tried to snag one off of the cooling rack, but they were still too hot.

He dropped it back onto the rack and turned quickly to run his fingertips under the water faucet.

"Serves you right," Jessica scolded him, "Did you not just see me putting another batch in? Where do you think these ones came from?"

He pouted at the back of Jessica's head.

Hope laughed and handed him a cookie that had cooled some but was still chewy and warm. Michael gave her a lopsided grin as Jessica shook her head and mumbled something about "coddling him".

"Kelsey would you like some?" Hope asked still laughing, and looking over at the grim looking girl who was hanging back in the hallway.

"No thank you," Kelsey replied quietly, nervously pushing her lank, black hair out of her eyes.

"How about some tea instead?"

"Tea would be great," Kelsey answered, smiling tentatively.

"That's the last batch," Jessica told them motioning toward the oven. Hope crossed the small kitchen and busied herself getting together all of the tea supplies.

"Anyone else want tea?" she asked, pulling two earthenware mugs from a cabinet.

"Sure," Jessica replied, but Michael shook his head no.

"Milk," he said with a mouthful of cookie.

"Your manners amaze me," Jessica said rolling her eyes. The women laughed, even Kelsey, and Michael frowned, shrugging his shoulders.

"You can both go sit in the living room," Jessica directed, handing Michael a gallon of milk from the fridge. "We're just going to clean up in here and we'll be right in."

Michael took the milk and then the mug Hope offered. He stood at the table and poured it himself. Kelsey rounded the corner and entered the small front room. She headed directly to the couch and sank down gratefully. She looked around the small room at photos of family, friends and a beautiful picture of the Blessed Mother with Jesus as a small baby in her arms. She sighed loudly.

Michael rounded the corner with his mug of milk and another two cookies, drawing Kelsey's attention away from the picture. He joined her on the couch, putting his cookies and milk on the side table next to where he sat. He glanced around for the remote and then stood quickly to retrieve it from where it sat next to the television. He clicked it on immediately and returned to the couch. He silently held out a cookie, but Kelsey shook her head. They continued to sit silently as Michael clicked through the television channels. The sound of Hope and Jessica banging around in the kitchen made Kelsey smile sadly as she remembered days when she and her mother used to do things like bake cookies together.

Finishing quickly, Jessica and Hope brought steaming mugs of tea and a plate full of cookies, into the living room.

"How are things with you?" Hope asked causally, handing Kelsey her mug of tea. "Be careful, it's hot."

"I'm okay," Kelsey said quietly, accepting the tea and stretching over the length of the sofa to set it on a coaster on the other small side table so it would cool .

"Kelsey, we want you to be able to come here and just relax – without being hammered with questions and things," Jessica told her settling onto the floor across from where Kelsey sat, holding her mug of tea in one hand and a cookie in the other. "But I just wanted to let you know that I was able to get you an appointment with my doctor for tomorrow at eleven thirty in the morning."

Michael nodded gratefully.

"Hope or I can take you there; you can go in alone or with either one of us," Jessica continued. "We just want you to do what's best to make you the most comfortable."

Kelsey looked from Jessica to Hope as her eyes filled with tears. "I don't know if you have any idea how grateful I am. I know I've been short and unfriendly to everyone that Michael has gotten to help me…" She spoke in a whisper.

Hope, who was still standing in the doorway, quickly set her mug down on the bookshelf and crouching down in front of Kelsey, took the girl's shaking hands.

Hope's dark brown eyes met Kelsey's hazel ones. She squeezed Kelsey's hands softly as Kelsey dropped her gaze. Hope let go of one of Kelsey's hands and stroked her cheek, ruddy with emotion, like a mother would.

"Listen honey," Hope told her gently, lifting Kelsey's chin with her hand. "We aren't angry with you."

Kelsey blinked her wide hazel eyes as one tear made it's way down her cheek. Hope brushed it aside gently.

"First off, we are complete strangers to you," Hope continued, lying her hand on Kelsey's leg. "And secondly, the bottom has fallen right out of your life."

Kelsey nodded in agreement.

"We don't expect you to be all hearts and flowers." Hope patted Kelsey's leg gently. "We just want you to know that we are here for you and that we truly, truly care about what's best for you. Any friend of Michael's is a friend of ours."

Kelsey took a deep breath and Hope let her go, leaning back on her heels, to give Kelsey some space.

"Yeah, but why do I get the feeling that you would do all this even if I were a complete stranger?" Kelsey asked, looking from Hope to Jessica.

"Because complete strangers need people to care about them too," Jessica told her simply. She held Kelsey's gaze as she took a sip of her tea and let the words sink in for a moment.

Hope sat down on the floor, pulling the elastic out and

letting her long dark hair flow straight down her back. She slid back and sat crossed-legged next to Jessica.

Michael stood up slowly and went to the bookcase. He snatched a tissue from the box next to Hope's tea. He saw Hope glancing up at her mug so he handed it down to her and then held the tissue out to Kelsey who took it and dabbed her eyes with it.

"After the appointment tomorrow," Michael said rubbing his hands on his thighs and smiling a small smile, "I think it's time to develop a game plan for Kelsey's next few months."

Hope and Jessica looked from Michael, who was nodding in response to their unasked question, to Kelsey who had lowered her head so her black hair hid her face which was blotchy from crying. Hope began to cry in relief. Jessica took Hope's hand and squeezed it tightly as their eyes met and they smiled together. They turned their attention back to Kelsey and waited in silence until she looked up.

"I'm so proud of you," Hope said softly, wiping away a tear with the back of her hand.

Jessica got up, absently adjusting the clip that held back her strawberry blonde hair. She leaned over to give Kelsey a long hug. She could feel Kelsey relax as she held her tightly. After a moment, Jessica let her go and knelt down in front of her as Hope slid up to sit in the recliner across from the couch.

"We all know that this is going to be a hard time for you and we want to support you in the best way that we can. You need to know that you can call us for anything at any time. We're here for you, sweet-heart," Jessica assured her, patting her on the leg gently.

Kelsey yawned.

"I'm so sorry," she stammered, covering her mouth quickly.

Jessica got up and tugged on Kelsey's hand to get her to

stand as well.

"You need to head to bed, " Jessica said. "No need to be sorry; there is plenty of time to talk and make plans."

Hope was getting to her feet and Michael was nodding in agreement.

Jessica walked Kelsey to Stevie's little bedroom and left her there to get ready for bed.

Hope and Michael had settled together onto the couch and were talking quietly but animatedly in the front room. Jessica could see from the hallway that they were both still smiling broadly. She turned back to the hall closet where she was looking for a wash-cloth and hand towel for Kelsey. She found a matching pair, which she handed to Kelsey as the girl came out of Stevie's room and turned into the bathroom.

Jessica moved back over to stand in the doorway where she could see the news clip on tv that had caught her attention.

"Good night," Kelsey called quietly, coming out of the bathroom and turning back into the small bedroom.

"Good night," Hope and Michael called back.

"All set?" Jessica asked, coming up behind Kelsey as she walked into Stevie's room.

"Yeah, I am," Kelsey replied, yawning again.

Jessica watched Kelsey slide under the covers, her long black hair fanning out behind her. Jessica pursed her lips. The poor girl looked exhausted.

"Jessica," Kelsey said quietly, "…thanks."

"It's my pleasure, Kelsey."

Jessica watched Kelsey shut her eyes and then she clicked off the light, saying a silent prayer. She walked down the narrow hall to join the on-going conversation in the living room.

"And on Sunday, I think we need to go and talk to her parents," Michael was saying to Hope, as Jessica sunk back onto the sofa on the other side of Michael.

"Did you two pray?" she asked.

The three of them immediately joined hands and offered a quiet prayer of thanksgiving to God for Kelsey's courage to see this pregnancy through. They also prayed in a special way for the new little baby — that one day God's light would shine through the new life Kelsey had growing inside of her.

"So Kelsey's folks still don't know?" Jessica asked quietly when the prayer had ended. She was absently rubbing her left eye.

Michael shook his head.

"How do you think that will go?" she asked, unclipping her hair and putting her feet up on the toy chest in front of her.

"Honestly, I have no idea," he replied, lines of worry creasing his handsome face.

Hope patted his forearm gently.

"I'm really worried about it," he admitted. "My gut tells me that they will try to pressure her to have an abortion. They tend to be the kind of people who will be concerned with what other folks are going to say."

"Well," Jessica cut in, "we'll be able to give Kelsey a place to stay so that she will not be in the spotlight."

"Stafford is certainly far enough away that she shouldn't run into anyone she knows out this way," Hope agreed.

Michael nodded, clenching his hands into fists. "I'm hopeful that if we approach Kelsey's parents with a plan already in place that makes this whole situation sound reasonable and well thought out, they will be more likely to respond positively."

"Is her mother going to be upset that she was not part of the planning process?" Jessica asked, rolling down the leg of her sweatpants. It was cooling off nicely in the house now that the oven had been turned off.

Michael thought for a moment, shielding his tired eyes with his hand .

"That's a real possibility, now that you mention it," he responded, blowing out a big breath and leaning back into the couch. He looked from Jessica to Hope and then turned to stare straight ahead.

Both women nodded thoughtfully.

"And how did your talk go with the youth group?" Hope inquired, turning to him and finishing the last bit of her tea.

"It actually went really well, I think," Michael told her.

His cell phone rang, interrupting them. He dug the phone out of his pocket and saw that it was Anna.

"It's Anna." A hint of pink heated his cheeks. "I bet Kelsey didn't call her," he said in quick explanation.

Both women nodded, determined not to smile.

"Hey Anna," Michael answered, wishing he could be swallowed by the couch.

Hope and Jessica stood at the same time to give Michael some privacy. They shared a knowing smile over his head and then quietly left the room talking of weekend plans as they went.

"Hi Michael. Have you heard from Kelsey today?" Anna asked, getting right to the heart of the matter.

"Yeah, I'm sorry," he apologized, running his hand back over his hair. "She's all set. We're both here at Jessica's and she's already asleep. I should have thought to call you."

"Oh no, that's no problem," Anna assured him. "I thought that was the plan for the weekend but I never heard anything concrete so I wanted to make sure that Kelsey got there okay."

"You're a great friend," Michael told her. He wondered if she could hear him smiling like some goofy teenager. "Oh, and I have some good news."

"Yeah?" she asked excitedly, "What's that?"

"Well, tomorrow, Kelsey is going to go to her first doctor's appointment," he replied.

"That's great," she responded.

Michael could hear her smile. It made him think of the way she would always sit back and observe things that gave her joy with a shy smile on her face.

"And then we're going to get together here and make some real plans for Kelsey's next couple of months."

"That's so wonderful, Michael! Thank God." Anna choked on her tears as she responded. "Is there anything else that I can do from here?"

"Just keep praying," he told her, "and also please thank your folks for me'"

"Will do," she replied, "Make sure that Kelsey knows she can call me if she needs anything."

"I will; thanks again, Anna. You've really helped Kelsey to make this decision. She talks about you quite a lot."

Anna smiled. "I'm thankful to be part of it."

"Talk to you tomorrow?" he asked, a little too quickly.

"Sure, call me after the appointment," she said.

"Will do. Talk to you then."

"Bye Michael."

Michael clicked the phone shut. He closed his eyes and leaned back into the couch for a moment. He could hear Jessica and Hope talking quietly in the kitchen. He wondered for a moment, if they were talking about him. Color heated his cheeks again as he stood up and looked around the corner to where the women sat across from one another at the kitchen table.

Jessica waved him in.

"Isn't Anna such a great girl?" she asked immediately.

Hope rolled her eyes as Michael, blushing scarlet, sat in the seat next to Jessica.

"Leave him alone," Hope warned, trying not to laugh herself.

Michael looked at Hope, ignoring Jessica who sat smiling sweetly in his direction.

"Anna is a great girl," he said emphatically, "but I'm sure that she sees me as a troublesome big brother."

Both women couldn't help but laugh.

"You have lots of time, Michael," Hope reminded him.

"Yeah, I know," he said, frowning slightly and looking away.

"Have you talked to Anna lately?" he asked turning back to his friends.

"She's got some Winter formal dance coming up at school," Hope remarked, as Jessica nodded. "She mentioned that she might like some help finding a dress."

Michael was immediately deflated. "So she's going then?"

"Well, I don't know about that," Hope told him. Jessica folded her hands and rested her chin on them watching the exchange silently.

"She never said that she was actually going... she just said that she would really like to go," Hope clarified.

"Has she talked to her parents about it yet?" he asked, fishing to see what they knew and absently peeling back the saran from another plate of cookies and helping himself to a peanut butter one.

"I don't know," Hope told him, "She didn't mention that to me when we talked.

He nodded his head.

Jessica reached over and tugged the saran back over the plate of cookies. "Why don't you offer to take her?" she asked smiling.

"Because if I did, and she really didn't want to go with me, she'd feel obligated..."he began, gesturing with the cookie in his hand.

Both women laughed again.

"You know Michael, she'd probably welcome the company," Jessica told him seriously. "I know her school crowd can be tough. It might be nice for her to have someone in the same ballpark to talk to for the evening."

Michael looked almost convinced. "But what would I say to Tim?"

"Why don't you just tell him the truth — you heard about the dance, you understand that Anna wants to go and you'd be happy to escort her there." Hope suggested.

"He'd probably be overjoyed to have you there to keep an eye on things," Jessica told him.

"Ugh!" he immediately responded, tossing the cookie onto the table. "See, that's what I mean! She's never going to take me seriously if she thinks that I'm an underground spy!"

"That's not what I mean," Jessica protested, as Michael glared at her angrily.

"Listen guys, it's late," Hope interjected, pushing back her chair. "I imagine that tomorrow will be another pretty emotional day. I think we should get some rest and then we can talk about this again tomorrow."

The three of them stood up.

"You're probably right," Jessica agreed, stretching her back.

"So I'm staying in the office?" Michael asked, turning to her, all anger vanished.

"Yeah, the cot is already set up in there for you," Hope told him, rounding the table and giving him a hug, "Good night all."

Hope hugged Jessica as well, and Michael made his way to the bathroom. Hope let herself out and crossed the backyard quickly, entering her own house.

Michael and Jessica took turns at the bathroom and in less than ten minutes, everyone had crawled into bed.

Michael was up by nine the next morning. He could never sleep in when he wasn't in his own bed. Kelsey and the women were wide awake and talking in the small kitchen. Everyone was sitting around the table, earthenware mug in hand.

Michael peered around the corner down the hallway and was happy to see the back of Kelsey's head. He did not like the idea of her seeing him first thing in the morning. He gave Jessica the high sign as he passed into the bathroom for a quick shower. As he towel-dried his short hair, he breathed in deeply. He felt like a whole new person. The stressful situation was beginning to take its toll and he could see worry lines on his face as he studied it in the small mirror above the sink. Turning quickly, he cracked open to door. The women were still seated around the kitchen table. He snuck back into the office, holding the towel tight around him. After drying quickly, he dressed and hung his towel up over the top side of the door. He grimaced suddenly – he had forgotten to bring his laundry basket. Now he would need to fit that in next week as well.

As Michael entered the kitchen, Hope got up quickly to give him her chair.

"Don't be silly," he protested.

"Where's your laundry?" she asked, moving away from the chair and draining her mug of coffee.

"I was just thinking about how I had forgotten it," he said pouting.

"Well, I need to throw a load in either way so you may as well sit here," she said. Michael took her seat as she headed to the counter to fix Michael a coffee.

"I'll be right back," she said, handing Michael his mug and turning to go out the door.

"So what's the plan for today?" Michael asked, holding the steaming mug to his nose. He breathed in the comforting sent of coffee.

"Jessica is going to take me to the appointment," Kelsey told him, absently running her finger around the top of her half empty coffee mug.

"Okay."

"And the strangest thing just happened," she talked right over him without realizing it. "I just got a phone call from one of the girls that I know from school. Her name is McKenna. She sounded all upset... said she needed to talk to me; that it was really important. I told her I was gone for the weekend and she just started sobbing."

Michael knit his brow together as she spoke. "What do you think is going on?" He looked to Jessica who sat impassively and then turned back to Kelsey.

"Maybe it's like you said," Kelsey suggested, "Maybe there's something up with McKenna."

"What are you going to do?" he asked, taking a drink from his mug.

"What can I do?" she retorted, fixing him with her hazel eyes. "I can call her back, but other than that, there isn't much that I can do from here."

Michael sighed. He did not like the idea of someone being in pain and far away. He looked back over at Jessica who still did not comment. He wasn't sure if Jessica knew what Kelsey was implying.

"I'm going to jump in the shower," she said instead, getting up and putting her mug into the sink.

"How well do you know her?" Michael pressed Kelsey, as Jessica headed down the hallway. "Could you convince her to tell you what is going on over the phone?"

"I can try, I guess," Kelsey responded reaching for her cell phone.

Michael got up and brought his coffee into the front

room. He did not want to seem like he was watching over Kelsey's shoulder. He flopped onto the couch and digging through the couch cushions, found the remote and clicked on the television.

The bathroom door opened and Jessica stuck her wet head out. "You used all the towels in here!" she hollered in his direction.

"Oh, sorry!"

Michael jumped up and rushed over to the hall closet to dig out some new towels. He opened the bathroom door a crack and passed two to Jessica who grabbed them and pulled the door shut quickly.

He could hear Kelsey pleading with McKenna over the phone as he stood at the closed door to the bathroom. He didn't want it to seem like he was ease-dropping so he turned around quickly.

"Thanks!" he heard Jessica holler through the door as he walked back into the front room. Flopping back onto the couch, he turned his attention to the television.

After another few moments, Kelsey rounded the corner and came over to where he laid on the couch. He moved quickly to a sitting position to make room for her. She looked as white as a sheet as she sank onto the couch next to him.

"What's up?" he asked, concerned.

"There's been some sort of an accident," Kelsey whispered, shading her eyes with a shaking hand.

"What kind of accident?" Michael pressed.

Kelsey licked her lips before continuing.

"Um, Adam was in an accident," she replied after a minute.

"Is he alright?! What kind of accident?!"

She nodded her head. "He's in the hospital. I guess he's pretty banged up. His car hit a tree."

134

Michael ran his hand through his almost dry hair. "Are you kidding?"

Kelsey looked at him blankly for a moment.

"You don't think…" she began, shaking her head.

"You think he may have done it on purpose?" he asked, immediately.

She hung her head so the black locks hid her face.

"I don't know," she whispered.

"Was he drinking?" Michael asked, hitting the mute button on the television.

"McKenna said she didn't know." Kelsey looked up at him, pushing the hair from in front of her face and fixing him with her hazel eyes.

The bathroom door clicked opened and Jessica came out fully dressed in jeans and a baby blue tee-shirt with her hair still wrapped up in a towel. She headed for her bedroom and both of them watched her go.

"Are you alright?" Michael asked, turning back to Kelsey after a few minutes of silence.

Kelsey nodded her head.

"I guess I don't care about him as much as I thought I did," she said suddenly.

"Why do you say that?" he asked.

"Because my first thought was — maybe now I won't have to give up the baby…" She looked away quickly as tears filler her eyes.

Michael took her hand and squeezed it gently. "You're probably just in shock, Kelsey," he told her quietly.

"I don't think I am," she replied, turning back to him. "I guess it's been made clear to me over the past week or so just what kind of guy Adam is. He's pretty spineless. That's probably not a nice thing to say about the poor guy, him being in the hospital and all."

Michael chuckled darkly. "Well, you never did pull any punches."

"I don't know, Michael. I don't know what I think."

Jessica appeared in the doorway of the living room. Her hair had been towel dried and pulled back into a pony-tail. It looked dark brown when it was wet.

"It looks awful serious in here," she remarked, leaning against the wall, not wanting to invade their space if they did not want her there.

"My boyfriend was in a car accident," Kelsey told her.

"Are you kidding?" Jessica asked incredulously, standing up to her full height. At 5'1" she looked serious, but not intimidating.

Kelsey shook her head.

"He's alright," Michael interjected. "At least, we think he's alright. He's in the hospital now."

"That's why your friend called all upset," Jessica surmised, coming into the room and sitting across from them in the recliner. "Is there someone else you can call for more information?"

"Should I call the hospital?" Kelsey asked.

"I wouldn't bother, they can't tell you anything over the phone any more...all these new privacy laws," Jessica said.

"Should I call my mom?" Kelsey asked.

"It's probably a good idea," Michael pointed out. "I mean, if she hears something from someone and doesn't know what is going on with you, she'll be even more worried."

"What should I say?"

"Just tell her that you decided to go out of town with some friends but you are fine and you wanted to tell her about the accident," he replied.

"Yeah, but I don't really have any information to give her," she said.

"Which you shouldn't since you are away with friends," Jessica reminded her.

Kelsey nodded her head. "Yeah, okay," she said standing up and walking back into the kitchen.

"What else, Jessica?" Michael asked frowning.

Jessica shook her head. She heard the back door opening, so she turned toward the sound.

"Hey!" Hope was calling, "Can I..." Hope stopped short when she saw that Kelsey was on the phone in the kitchen.

"Sorry," she said softly.

Jessica, who had stuck her head around the corner from the front room, motioned for Hope to come all the way through the kitchen. Hope rounded the corner and Jessica explained what was going on.

Hope was shaking her head sadly when Kelsey came back into the room.

"Things cool with your mom?" Jessica asked.

Kelsey shrugged. "Can I shower now?"

"Yeah, go ahead," Jessica replied.

Hope stepped into the hall in front of Kelsey and opened the hall closet. She pulled out a clean towel and handed it to Kelsey, who was passing through to the bedroom to get a change of clothes.

"Thanks," Kelsey murmured. Turning to Jessica she asked, "How soon do we have to leave?"

"In about forty-five minutes."

Kelsey nodded and went first into the bedroom and then to take her turn in the bathroom.

Hope returned to sit with Michael and Jessica in the living room.

"Some weird stuff going on," he observed.

"Was he drinking?" Hope asked, leaning her small frame against the wall.

"Kelsey doesn't really have any information," he replied. "She made a comment though which makes me think that she might believe this accident happened on purpose."

"Really?" Jessica asked surprised.

"He hasn't handled the news of the baby particularly well," Michael explained.

"But to try to take his own life?" Jessica asked. "Is that what you think?"

"I'm not saying that's what's going on," Michael interrupted, "I'm just saying that Kelsey thought it was a bit weird... the timing and all. And she told me the other day that if his parents found out they would force Adam to marry her. She said neither she nor Adam wanted that."

Hope crossed her arms and nodded her head. "I can understand why he's upset. Did Kelsey tell him that she intended to have the baby?"

"I don't know the answer to that question," Michael replied, "It seemed to me that she had pretty much just made the decision yesterday, but I could be wrong about that. Maybe she said something to Adam before she left school for the weekend."

"Do you think that he might have thought that if she was definitely set on having the baby that there was no way to keep it a secret from his parents? Jessica asked, pushing up the sleeves of her long-sleeve tee-shirt.

"Makes sense," Hope remarked, sliding down the wall and wrapping her arms around her bent knees.

"I'll have to ask Kelsey about it when she gets out of the shower," Michael said.

"Or I can ask her when I take her out to the doctor's appointment," Jessica suggested.

"Yeah, why don't you then," Michael agreed, turning his attention to the television. "I think I need a break from being the shrink for a while."

Hope and Jessica talked softly of other things. Michael didn't even hear them. He continued to zone out and pay attention to the television.

After a while, the bathroom door opened and Kelsey came out. She was dressed in white jeans with black Gothic print down one leg. She clutched her oversize black hoodie tight at the middle and her hair hung limply down her back.

"Right on time," Jessica remarked, standing up.

"Time to go already?" There was just a hint of fear in Kelsey's voice as she asked the question. She still held a damp towel in her hand.

"No worries," Michael told her standing up quickly. He came to where she stood and took the towel out of her hand. He handed it back to Hope. Leaning down, he gave Kelsey a tight squeeze. "Jessica will be with you the whole time," he reminded her. "She'll keep an eye on things."

Kelsey nodded.

"Are we going to your parent's tomorrow?" Michael asked before letting her go.

Kelsey shrugged.

"You may as well get it over with," Hope suggested. "Believe me when I tell you that you'll feel better after putting that step behind you."

Kelsey looked over at her. Hope was shaking the towel out but watching Kelsey.

"Probably," she agreed grudgingly, "by Monday I should be a whole new person."

The room laughed together.

"Grab your purse and then we'll go," Jessica told Kelsey, who headed back into the room she slept in and came back carrying her small black purse.

"See you guys in a while," Jessica said, grabbing Kelsey's

hand and leading her toward the back door.

"What are you gonna do now?" Michael asked Hope after Jessica and Kelsey walked out of the house.

"I'm going to finally finish some laundry," she replied. "And I have other laundry at home that still needs to be folded."

"Need help?" Michael asked.

"If you're offering," she answered.

Michael followed Hope out of Jessica's house and across the yard, into her own small home. The layout of both homes was similar and Michael followed Hope to the basement where she had set up a folding table and was organizing all the laundry by owner.

"You have tons of clothes here," he observed.

"What do you expect from a street full of women? Poor Stevie, he doesn't have a chance!"

They laughed easily.

"You mean, you do everyone's laundry?" Michael asked, folding a tee-shirt that belonged to a child smaller than Hope's girls.

"Yeah, each one of us has our assigned chores. Martha handles yard work, Jessica mops and cleans bathrooms and I do laundry and shopping."

Michael nodded his head in wonder. "Sounds like some set-up you have here."

"It works for us," Hope told him. "So tell me about your talk last night." She motioned for Michael to take a seat.

"Well, you know what," Michael said settling onto a small sofa in the finished basement, "I prayed for a good part of the afternoon. I was pretty concerned about speaking because I thought someone would bring up the situation about St. Monica's."

Hope nodded as she deftly made her way through the laundry pile.

"I considered calling Fr. John or Deacon Thomas but instead I grabbed out the Catechism and did some reading."

"I'm impressed," Hope said smiling. She pushed a strand of dark hair back over her ear.

Michael made a face at her and then continued, "You know what I realized? It is on the conscience of the communicant whether or not they are in a position to receive the Eucharist."

"That still doesn't address the idea of handing it out like candy," Hope protested, folding a small pair of jeans.

"No, you're right, it doesn't," Michael agreed. "But one of the things that I shared with the kids last night was the importance of learning and spreading the true faith — that which was handed down to us by the apostles. That's part of our calling, Hope, once we are baptized." Michael leaned forward and studied her closely.

She stopped folding and watched him steadily.

"I'm never going to church at St. Monica's again," Michael replied, "not until that Pastor leaves. As for the Warners... I'm just going to keep on praying for Tim's discernment."

"Well, I'll say we have our work cut out for us — explaining to the good folks of this geographic area, why we don't agree with what's happening at St. Monica's," she said, taking up another pair of jeans and folding them quickly.

"You know what the best part was of last night?" Michael asked her. She could hear the enthusiasm in his voice and she stopped folding again to give him her full attention. "It was talking to those kids about John 6. It's like they had never heard it before."

Michael leaned back on the sofa, holding up his hands as if to signify stop.

"They probably hadn't," Hope remarked seriously.

"I know, but they were so hungry for the truth." Michael rubbed his hands together. " It's almost like I could see the light bulbs turning on as I spoke."

"Well, this situation will give us new ground to cover in that respect," she said thoughtfully.

"So we make the best of it," he stated. "I say we challenge each person at our parishes to discuss what's going on at St. Monica's. Imagine all the folks we'll be able to talk to that way?!"

Hope laughed at his eagerness. "Well, you have me convinced, but I think it might be better if we started distributing information first. We don't want to scare everyone away. I think something on paper is much more charitable."

Michael pouted. "I suppose," he agreed, finally.

Great! Let me grab my laptop and you can get started writing something!"

CHAPTER EIGHT
Stricken

Kelsey was glad that Jessica was with her at the Doctor's office. First of all, Jessica helped Kelsey to fill out the mound of paperwork that the receptionist handed her when Kelsey checked in at the window.

Jessica could see Kelsey's hand shaking slightly as she began looking through the forms. Kelsey asked Jessica a few questions about medical terms that she did not understand.

The large wooden door opened suddenly, causing both of the women in the waiting room to jump.

"Kelsey Springer?" a middle-aged blond haired nurse asked with a smile.

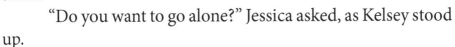

"Do you want to go alone?" Jessica asked, as Kelsey stood up.

Kelsey thought a moment.

"You can come in later, if she needs you," the nurse told them both pleasantly.

"I'll go alone for now," Kelsey said, following the nurse through the open door.

Jessica nodded her head and sat back in the waiting room chair. She glanced at the small sign that showed the picture of a cellphone with a large red "x" through it and she frowned. She grabbed her purse and stood quickly.

Walking up to the small window, she waited to get the

attention of the woman behind the computer screen.

Sliding the window to the side, the receptionist asked pleasantly, "How can I help you?"

"I'm just going out the door to make a quick call," Jessica explained.

The woman looked at her questioningly.

"In case Kelsey needs me."

The receptionist smiled, "Of course."

Jessica stepped out onto the sidewalk and dug though her purse for her phone. Grabbing it out, she text a quick message to Michael and Anna, letting them know it was time to pray because Kelsey had gone into the doctor's office She placed a quick call to Hope and then to Martha, who was still away visiting her mother. After finishing, Jessica unwound the cord Rosary from around her wrist and began reciting a prayer of Thanksgiving that they had managed to get this far. She pulled open the entrance door to the doctor's office and returned to the same seat she had been sitting in before. The receptionist noticed her walk back in and she smiled pleasantly.

Jessica sat in the chair, leaning forward with her elbows on her knees and she prayed the Rosary fervently. After about twenty minutes, the same middle-aged, blonde nurse opened the door to the waiting room. She glanced around and saw Jessica sitting in the same seat as before. Since there were now others waiting along with her, the nurse walked quietly over to where Jessica sat and leaning down said softly, "Kelsey would like you to come in now."

Jessica nodded, standing quickly. She followed the nurse down a short hallway. The nurse stopped in front of a shut door. She knocked softly and then opened the door to let Jessica in.

The nurse followed her into the small exam room and motioned for her to take the empty seat near the door.

"Hello, Jessica," Dr. Wilkes said as Jessica sat. The doctor was a handsome looking older gentleman with graying hair and glasses. He had a gentle demeanor and strong hands. He spoke quietly and with a sincere concern. Jessica was thankful to have found him.

"Hi Doctor," Jessica replied, smiling.

Kelsey was already lying on the exam table in a paper exam gown.

"Kelsey wanted you to come in because I have asked her to allow me to do an internal examination. I would like to see how far along she is for certain," Dr. Wilkes explained.

Jessica nodded her head. "Where should I go?" she asked.

"Why don't you take that seat you're in and pull it up to Kelsey's side," the doctor suggested.

Jessica did as she was instructed.

"How're you doing?" she asked Kelsey, as the doctor washed his hands and put on his exam gloves.

"Okay," Kelsey replied, "But the last time I had an exam like this it hurt terribly." She reached out for Jessica's hand.

"He'll explain everything that he's going to do to you, Kelsey," Jessica promised. taking her hand and squeezing it softly.

Dr. Wilkes stood over Kelsey. He rested his hand slightly on her forearm and said, "First, let me explain to you what an internal exam is and why I'm going to perform one on you."

Jessica squeezed Kelsey's hand and the young girl glanced at her with a small smile. Jessica said another quick prayer of Thanksgiving for having found such a wonderful doctor.

After explaining the procedure, the doctor began the examination. From her vantage point, Jessica could tell that something was making him uneasy.

Kelsey shifted on the table, squeezing Jessica's hand tighter and Dr. Wilkes said, "I'm sorry Kelsey, if this is uncomfortable for you. I will be finished here in just a few moments."

Dr. Wilkes turned away from his patient, stripped off his gloves and washed his hands again. The nurse motioned for Kelsey to sit up.

"Let me give you a moment to dress and then I'll come back," the doctor said as he and the nurse turned toward the door.

"I'll wait outside as well," Jessica said, following them both out of the small room.

"Is everything alright, Doctor?" Jessica asked.

Dr. Wilkes looked thoughtful for a few moments and then responded, "Actually Jessica, I am going to order an ultrasound for Kelsey."

Jessica searched his eyes with concern. "An ultrasound? Isn't that procedure?" she asked.

The doctor did not respond, but instead knocked quietly on the door.

"All set," Kelsey called from the exam room.

Dr. Wilkes entered, holding the door for Jessica.

"Do you want me to come in?" Jessica asked, peering into the room at Kelsey who nodded.

"Kelsey," Dr. Wilkes began, "I am going to order an ultrasound for you."

"Okay," Kelsey said, her brows knitting with concern, "Isn't an ultra-sound normal?"

Jessica went to stand over next to Kelsey. She put her arm around Kelsey's shoulder and rubbed her arm vigorously.

"An ultrasound is a routine procedure which can be done here in the office. I would like to see how far along you are, and an ultrasound is just the thing," the doctor explained.

"Is there something wrong?" Kelsey asked shivering. She could hear something unsaid in the doctor's voice and she felt uneasy.

Jessica held her a little tighter and waited for the doctor to respond.

"I don't know the answer to that yet, Kelsey. Your uterus is not developing the way that it should for someone who is about two or three months pregnant. The pregnancy test has come back positive, which means that you have pregnancy hormones in your system. I would like to take a good look at what is going on in there," Dr. Wilkes said.

Kelsey did not respond right away. She clutched her hoodie tighter and looked over at Jessica who said nothing but continued to hold her hand.

"What if something is wrong?" she asked finally.

Dr. Wilkes put his hand on her knee and looked at her seriously.

"First we need to see what the issues are and then we will decide how to deal with them," he assured her. "I know that you are upset... you have been upset about this pregnancy for some time. Let me order this ultrasound so we will have all of the facts so that we can make the best decisions we can for you."

"Can you do that right here in the office, doctor?" Jessica asked.

Dr. Wilkes nodded. "Yes, there's an ultrasound machine at the end of the hall on the right."

Turning to Kelsey he said, "You will need to drink about a liter of water. I'll have the nurse bring it to you here. When you are finished, you can head down to the ultrasound room, just let the nurse know when you are going. Have you ever had an ultrasound before?"

"Actually yes," Kelsey replied, "I had mono when I was in high school and they were checking my spleen."

"So you know all about ultrasounds?" the doctor asked smiling. He turned to write something in Kelsey's chart.

"Yes, I do," she replied.

"Okay then, I'll send the nurse in here with the water. When you are done, just let her know and head down to the ultra-sound room," Dr. Wilkes said, opening the door and motioning to one of the nurses.

The nurse returned a moment later with a plastic cup and two pitchers of water. She placed them on the counter.

"Just let me know when you are finished," she said softly, letting herself out of the small exam room.

Jessica moved to hand Kelsey the first cup of water. Kelsey took it, without seeing and drank from it mechanically. Jessica leaned against the exam table and rubbed Kelsey's back. The young girl was close to tears, but she held fast and did not cry.

"What do you think is wrong?" Kelsey asked, meeting Jessica's deep blue eyes.

"I don't know, honey," Jessica said softly. She turned to stand in front of Kelsey. She pushed the black hair out of her face and gave her should a tight squeeze.

Kelsey sighed deeply as Jessica turned and leaned back against the table again.

"This is totally out of control," Kelsey said after finishing her first cup of water.

Jessica poured a second as Kelsey continued, "Last week I'd have given anything not to be pregnant and now — this minute, I'm panicking because something isn't right."

"Let's just see what the doctor has to say before any one starts to panic," Jessica suggested. "Do you want to pray?"

Kelsey pretended not to have heard her. She looked away from where Jessica stood and studied the old movie posters which were decorating one of the walls.

Jessica bowed her head silently and offered up her own prayer. Kelsey slid off the exam table to refill her own cup. Jessica glanced at the clock, knowing that the more time that passed without her contacting Hope, the greater the concern would be at the house that something wasn't right. She looked at Kelsey who was steadily drinking with her back to her, but she couldn't bear to leave the girl alone.

"I feel awful," Kelsey complained.

"I know," Jessica agreed, "it's lousy. The quicker you finish, the faster we can get on with it."

Kelsey grimaced and downed another cup which finished off her first pitcher of water.

"I just don't understand," Kelsey said again, pouring from the full pitcher.

"Don't try to right now," Jessica said softly, fingering her Rosary in one hand, and taking Kelsey's hand in her other. She squeezed it softly.

It took another half hour for Kelsey to finish the second pitcher of water. As soon as she put the last cup down, Jessica was opening the door, glancing up and down the hall, searching for the nurse. She caught her coming out of another exam room a few doors away. The nurse nodded in understanding as Jessica led Kelsey down the hall to the last room on the right.

They opened the exam room door and a tall college-aged guy looked up at them from his perch next to the ultrasound machine.

"Hi," the guy said pleasantly, "I'm Alex. Dr. Wilkes has ordered an ultrasound for you. Please lie back on the table."

Jessica helped Kelsey settle back on the pillow.

Alex briefly explained what he was going to do.

"Should she be in an exam gown?" Jessica asked when he was finished speaking.

"That's alright, her over-sized sweatshirt will be easy enough to maneuver," Alex replied, folding back the fabric to expose Kelsey's abdomen.

In a few moments, the procedure was completed.

Alex opened the door far enough to let them both pass.

"She's all set for now," Alex explained to Jessica. "Go ahead and wait in the waiting room. I need to review this information with Dr. Wilkes and then he will be with you again shortly."

Kelsey started to cry quietly as she and Jessica walked down the hallway in one direction and Alex went in the other.

"I don't understand what's wrong," she told Jessica sadly.

Jessica took Kelsey's hand gently and led her through the door and back to the waiting room. Mercifully, it was empty. Jessica began to finger her Rosary again as Kelsey tried to distract herself by looking through a Home and Garden magazine. They had been at the doctor's office well past lunch time.

After ten minutes, which felt more like ten hours, the blonde nurse opened the door and called Kelsey and Jessica to follow her. They both stood slowly. She led them back into the same small exam room. This time the nurse did not stay, but shut the door quietly after letting them in.

Almost immediately, they were joined by Dr. Wilkes.

"What's wrong?" Jessica asked the doctor, she she stood next to Kelsey who was sitting back on the exam table.

"Well, it appears that Kelsey isn't pregnant after all," Dr. Wilkes said gently.

No one said a word.

"How is that possible?" Jessica asked after a few minutes. Kelsey turned to stare at the wall.

"Honestly, Jessica and Kelsey, I have no idea how it is possible," the doctor replied baffled. " I have some theories but I don't know for sure. Kelsey, will you allow me to do a blood test which will also check your pregnancy hormone levels?"

"Is it possible that she lost the baby?" Jessica asked, trying to make sense of this new scenario.

The doctor looked at Kelsey kindly and asked, "Have you had any spotting or bleeding of any kind?"

She shook her head.

Turning slowly to face him, she said, "No, nothing. That's the reason why I thought I was pregnant in the first place."

"Of course, that would be the most logical explanation," the doctor said. It was clear that he was thinking out loud.

"Is Kelsey otherwise healthy?" Jessica asked concerned.

"I would like to do more blood work," the doctor began, ticking things off on his fingers. "There needs to be some explanation for Kelsey's hormone levels. We need to figure out what that is…. Kelsey, what form of birth control were you using when you got pregnant?"

"I haven't taken a pill since I first realized I had missed a period," she responded quietly.

"Tell me about that," the doctor said, motioning for Jessica to resume her seat next to the exam table. He lowered himself onto the small stool and gave Kelsey his full attention.

"Well, I just finished the package…" she explained. "I never have taken the placebo pills — it just always seemed stupid to me. And I waited to get my period and I never did. When the seven days were over and I still hadn't gotten my period, I waited some more. I didn't start the next packet of pills because I was scared to. I felt like the only reason I would miss was because I was pregnant. And it was right after the one time that Adam and I…"

Kelsey turned away quickly.

"And why were you prescribed birth control to begin with?" Dr. Wilkes asked. "You said you weren't sexually active when you first got them." It appeared that he was reviewing the information from Kelsey's chart.

"When I arrived on campus, I was having issues with cramps and I had missed some time in class. One of my professors suggested that I go to the infirmary and speak to the doctor there. He's the one who prescribed the birth control pills," she explained. "I started taking them. The first month I had horrible cramps that put me in bed for three days. I went back to the infirmary and they told me that sometimes that happens when the body is getting used to the dosage and the hormones."

Jessica shook her head angrily.

"The next month, the cramps were so mild, I couldn't believe it and then from then on, I never had another cramp again. And the best part was that I could sometimes control when I was going to get my period – like if I had to do marching band… our uniforms had white pants. I hated having my period when there was a game," Kelsey explained.

"Do you think this is connected to the birth control pills?" Jessica asked.

Dr. Wilkes stood up slowly.

"I don't know the answer to that," he said honestly. "I really believe it would be best to do some more tests. How do you feel about that, Kelsey?"

Kelsey remained silent for a few minutes.

"I know that you are in school away from here," Dr. Wilkes told her. "I would even be willing to come into the office tomorrow to get some blood work started if you would rather not do anything more today."

"Blood work is fine," Kelsey said flatly. "And we can do it today…I mean, I'm already here."

"Okay then, I will send in the nurse to draw your blood. Depending upon the results of these tests, I may need to have you come back and do another round of blood work after fasting for 24 hours," the doctor told her.

Kelsey nodded in understanding.

"I have only one request Kelsey," he said urgently. "Do

not go back to the doctor at the infirmary, unless you are ill, and refrain from taking any more pills or engaging in any more acts of a sexual nature until we're able to figure out what's going on here."

Kelsey nodded again.

"I feel this is important to pursue," he told her gently, placing a hand on her shoulder. "I believe we need to get to the bottom of this as quickly as we can."

Dr. Wilkes squeezed her shoulder and turned to leave. He left the door ajar so that the nurse could enter.

"Do you want me to stay?" Jessica asked gently as Kelsey gazed past her to the pictures on the wall.

Kelsey just nodded and let go of Jessica's hand.

"Do you feel okay?" Jessica asked quietly, after a few moments of silence.

Kelsey shrugged.

"Guess this explains why I never felt sick," she said, "I was just talking to Michael about that last night."

Jessica didn't respond. She pulled the sleeves down on her shirt. The temperature in the room seemed to go down a couple of degrees.

"Jessica, do you think there's something wrong with me?" Kelsey asked, her eyes welling up with tears.

Jessica stood quickly and pulled Kelsey into a tight hug as the began sobbing against her chest.

"Oh honey," Jessica said soothingly, "this isn't your fault."

The door opened quietly and the same blonde nurse came in carrying a small plastic box with everything needed for drawing blood. She stood to the side and did not interrupt. She and Jessica exchanged a look of compassion as Kelsey cried herself out. Noticing the nurse had entered the room, Kelsey straightened up stiffly and wiped her eyes with the back of her hand.

"Sorry," she mumbled.

"There's no need to be sorry, sweetheart," the nurse said quietly, "you just take the time you need to grieve this situation. You'll be a better person for it."

Kelsey did not respond.

Jessica stepped back to give the nurse some space.

"My name is Maggie. I'm going to take a couple of vials of blood and then you will be all set here," the nurse said, "Have you ever had blood drawn before?"

Kelsey nodded her head.

"Why don't we move this chair over there?" The nurse motioned to an empty space by a small counter.

Kelsey hopped off the exam table and Jessica moved the chair to the place the nurse had indicated. In another few moments, Maggie had gotten all the blood she needed and was gently putting a bandage on Kelsey's arm.

"I'll pray for you tonight, sweetheart," the nurse said quietly as she gazed down into Kelsey's sad face, "You're all set here. It will be mid-week by the time we get the results from these tests. Dr. Wilkes said he will call you personally as soon as they arrive."

The nurse left the door ajar on her way out and Kelsey got wearily up from the chair. She walked past Jessica and slowly back out the way that she had come in. Jessica let her lead. After passing into the waiting room, Jessica stopped at the front desk and spoke to the receptionist for a moment, then she turned to follow Kelsey out to the car.

"Back to the house?" Jessica asked, before turning the key in the ignition.

"Why do I feel so bad?" Kelsey asked her, leaning back against the passenger seat and closing her eyes. "I feel like someone has died."

"In a way, someone has," Jessica told her. "Kelsey, you

came here, fully expecting to find out more about a new little baby inside you; one that you had made the decision to carry to term. Now that the situation is different, that is a great loss for you. Don't feel bad about feeling bad."

Kelsey let out a big sigh and continued sitting against the seat, eyes closed tightly.

"Let's get back to the house and take some time to let the dust settle on this news," Jessica suggested starting the car.

Kelsey remained silent, either looking away out the window or learning back with her eyes shut, the whole way home.

Hope knew immediately that something was horribly wrong as soon as Jessica got out of the car. She shut the door and went quickly around, helping Kelsey to get out of her side. Hope and Michael exchanged a glance as they continued to watch from the window.

"This is real bad," Hope murmured, looking at Kelsey's stricken face as Jessica led her to the back door. Michael and Hope moved farther back into the kitchen.

As soon as Kelsey set foot in the house, she began to sob inconsolably. Michael reached out for her, but she batted his hand away and ran back to Stevie's room where she had spent the night before.

With Kelsey gone from the room, Jessica sank into a chair at the kitchen table and put her head down on her hands. Michael stood in silence, not knowing what to say or do next. He could hear Kelsey still sobbing down the short hallway. Jessica had also started to cry in the kitchen. He glanced from one sound to the other uncertainly.

The beep of the microwave startled him and he looked over to see Hope pulling out two mugs of steaming hot tea. She set them both down on the counter.

"How does Kelsey take her tea?" she asked Michael, pulling open the fridge to get the milk.

"Um... I dunno," he replied uncertainly, watching Jessica cry at the table.

"Michael," Hope demanded his full attention. "How does Kelsey take her tea?"

"Uh…cream and sugar, I think," he replied uneasily, looking at her directly.

Hope fixed both cups of tea. One she placed softly on the table near Jessica and the other she carried with her into the hallway.

"Kelsey, I have some tea for you," she said gently, knocking on the door. Immediately, the sobbing stopped.

Waiting a moment and getting no response, she opened the door a small crack. "I'm just going to put this down on the bookshelf and you can have it when you are ready."

Kelsey looked up at her with a tear streaked face. She still did not respond.

Hope set the tea down. She waited a moment to see if Kelsey would speak and when Kelsey turned away, Hope left the room, shutting the door quietly behind her.

Michael was sitting across from Jessica at the kitchen table holding both of her hands as she cried quietly. Hope sank into the seat next to them.

"We waited for you," he told Hope.

"So, there's no baby," Jessica said quietly, releasing Michael's hands and cupping her mug of tea.

"What do you mean, no baby?" Michael asked clearly confused.

"Dr. Wilkes ordered an ultrasound after he did an internal exam," she began, "just to make sure."

"Well, what's going on?" Hope asked confused.

"I don't know the answer to that," Jessica said, looking

156

directly at her friend.

No one said anything for a moment.

"What I do know is that there is no baby growing in Kelsey's uterus," Jessica said.

"I don't understand," Michael said breathlessly, "the pregnancy tests…"

Jessica nodded and took a tissue that Hope had plucked from the box on the counter.

"All of the hormone tests were positive, even the ones at the doctor's office," Jessica said. She pulled the elastic out of her strawberry blonde hair which had long since dried. She shook it out and rubbed her temples with both hands. She shut her eyes.

"What does this mean?" Hope asked.

"They don't really know what it means," Jessica replied, opening her blue eyes and looking directly into Hope's brown ones. "After the ultrasound, the doctor ordered some blood work. The nurse took five vials but the results won't be available until sometime mid-week."

"Uh, should I go check on Kelsey?" Michael asked irritably. He felt excluded from their conversation.

"I think you should let her be for now," Hope responded, glancing in his direction.

He shifted uneasily in his seat and ran a hand over his short hair.

"I'm worried," Jessica said finally. The others waited for her to finish. "The doctor was talking about birth control pills that Kelsey had been on; he seemed confused and upset as well. Almost like he's never seen such a thing before…"

"What do you think that means?" Hope asked again.

Michael stood up quickly. He headed toward the back door. He needed to get some air and he did not want to sit in on all the speculative talk that would be occurring. The conversation broke off while he moved through the kitchen. He went out the door and walked through the yard to where there sat a hammock hanging from two trees. It had been hung by the previous owner and no one had ever taken it down. It was frayed around the edges. Jessica, Hope and Martha talked often of replacing it, but no one ever had. Michael sat on the hammock which almost touched the ground under his body weight. He looked toward the window of Stephen's room. He knew that Kelsey was in there and he knew that she was devastated. He wondered what this would mean for her future.

The door opened suddenly and Hope leaned outside shaking his cell phone from side to side. "Your father," she called into the still day.

"I'll call him back," Michael responded.

She went back inside, taking the cell phone with her.

Michael thought for a few moments about his father; about his work with genetics research. Michael would have to explain this whole situation to him. He cringed thinking about how his father would relish the scientific side of things. That was one of the things that bothered Michael the most. He felt like his father always thought like a scientist first and a person later. It would be good however to have his input on this very strange circumstance. Michael pushed off with his foot and laid back in the hammock as it swung gently from side to side.

The back door opened again a short time later. Michael opened his eyes and saw it was Kelsey who stepped wearily out the door. She had changed into sweatpants and had tied her dark hair up in a bun. She looked like the walking dead.

Michael swung up to a sitting position. He gripped the hammock as if to stand, but forced himself to remain sitting. Perhaps she was just looking to get some air also and didn't intend to speak with him. Kelsey stood on the porch and looked out over the small yard. She spied Michael sitting on the hammock and gave him a small wave. He waved back to her and she left the porch, walking in his direction.

"Are you feeling okay?" he asked with concern as she approached. He stood up quickly offering her the hammock. He wanted to reach for her but wasn't sure if he should. They stood awkwardly for a moment until Kelsey leaned over to get into the hammock.

Michael held it steady as she sank down onto the woven ropes. She looked tired and drawn.

"Yeah," she said flatly, "I feel fine. I've felt fine all along."

Michael did not respond. He was not too sure what to say. Kelsey kicked a small pile of dirt that marked the spot where people's feet hung when they sat in the hammock.

"It's weird really," Kelsey remarked, smoothing back the stray strands of her hair, "last week I would have paid any amount of money to make this pregnancy thing go away. Now it has and I feel all empty inside

Michael leaned his back against the tree.

"I think that's probably normal," he said softly, chancing a reply.

"What if there's something really seriously wrong with me, Michael? " she asked, her hazel eyes wide. "What if I'm going to die?"

Michael did not respond right way.

"What do you think happens when you die, Kelsey? Are you afraid of it?"

She looked at him wearily, sorry she had said anything.

"Of course I'm afraid," she snapped, after a moment.

They remained silent for a few moments.

"What I'm most afraid of though is not being here," she said finally, "not existing in this place...and what about my family?"

"I honestly believe Kelsey — that people who die live on

in eternity."

She rolled her eyes.

"I know you aren't interested in a big theological discussion right now," he told her, meeting her hazel eyes with his blue ones, "but I'm afraid too of not existing in this place any more either. But I temper that fear with the idea that there is some where better to exist. And that somewhere is heaven."

"I wouldn't even know if I'm going to heaven," she said quietly.

Michael remained quiet. "You'd get there eventually," he said.

"Are you talking about purgatory?" she asked him.

He smiled but didn't reply.

"Look at my life, it's a mess," she pointed out. "I slept with my boyfriend, I don't go to church any more, I never pray. God wouldn't want me."

Michael crouched down and took one of Kelsey's hands in his.

"God always wants you, Kelsey."

She bowed her head and cried some more.

"How can I still be crying?"

"You know the Catechism, Kelsey, even if you want to pretend that you don't. You know how to fix those things that are holding you back from God."

She turned away from him, trying to pull her hand from his grasp. He held to it firmly

"When is the last time you went to confession?"

Kelsey looked over at him tears streaking her cheeks. "I can't even remember."

"I can set something up for you with one phone call," Michael told her, squeezing her hand tightly. "Just give me the word."

"Can I think about it?" she asked tired from the emotion

160

of the day.

"Of course you can."

Michael let go of her hand and stood back up.

"Did you see Jessica and Hope?" he asked her.

She sniffled and pulled a tissue out of the pocket of her sweatshirt.

"Yeah, they haven't said anything, but they are both acting like two old worried hens…"

Her metaphor made Michael laugh. "They are just concerned about you."

She smiled as she dried her tears. "Yeah, I know. You know some pretty special people, Michael."

He nodded in agreement. "Do you want to go back inside?"

"I think that I would like to stay here for a few minutes," she said, lying back onto the hammock and closing her eyes to the world. "Is that okay?"

"Sure thing; I'm going to go in and see about checking my email." Michael turned and walked down the long yard. He could hear the squeak as the hammock swayed slightly and he smiled.

Michael flipped open his phone as soon as he grabbed it off of the kitchen counter. "Jessica?" he called.

"Office," Jessica called back.

"I need the number of a good priest in the area," he said, walking hurriedly down the short hall.

Jessica grabbed her worn address book from the shelf next to her computer and flipped it open. Michael hung around the corner, watching her.

"Where's Hope?" he asked.

Leafing through the pages Jessica stopped at one and scanned down to the middle of the page.

"She went back home to give Kelsey some space."

Pointing to a number she said, "Father Gregory Mary. Call his cell because you might not get him at the rectory this late on a Saturday afternoon."

"What time is their vigil mass?" Michael asked, balancing the book with one hand and punching in numbers with the other.

"5:30."

Michael turned and left the room, going instead to Jessica's bedroom and shutting the door behind him. Fr. Gregory Mary picked up on the second ring. Michael explained, as briefly as he could, about the situation with Kelsey. Father was willing to give him a window of opportunity from four o'clock until five fifteen — he could be found at the rectory before Mass — and he thought it was as important as possible to get Kelsey to confession and Mass in the same day. Michael agreed to call ahead if they were going to make it. He flipped the phone shut and bowed his head to say a short prayer.

Michael looked at his phone intently and then picked it back up to call his father.

"Hello Dad," Michael said.

"Michael!" his father said in his gruff voice, sounding in a hurry, "I'm so glad that you called me back."

"Is everything alright?" Michael asked. "Are you busy?"

"I wanted to talk to you about our last phone conversation," Patrick explained.

"What about it?" Michael asked.

"Well, we've been doing some additional research and it seems to be a bit more complicated than I first thought."

"What does that mean?" Michael asked.

"Those cluster pregnancies I was telling you about ..."

"Yeah?"

"Over ninety percent of them have major complications," Patrick said.

Michael was silent.

"Michael, are you there?"

"Yeah, yeah, I'm here," Michael responded.

"Is everything okay with Kelsey?" Patrick pressed.

"Well, actually, no…but the doctor has no idea what is going on other than the fact that she isn't really pregnant," Michael said. "I'm sorry Dad, but I really don't have any other details than that. I know they are doing more tests and stuff."

"Who is the doctor?" Patrick asked.

"Jessica's doctor; I don't remember the name. Do you want me to get you the number?" Michael asked him.

"If you could, that would be great. I would love to discuss with him some of our findings."

"And Dad…" Michael said. "When you say major complications…"

"The complications have been with the babies, not with the mothers," Patrick told him.

Michael nodded, understanding his qualifying statement.

"And if you could get me that information soon," Patrick urged.

"I'll get right on it," Michael promised, "Thanks for calling me, Dad."

"I love you, Son."

"Love you too, Dad."

CHAPTER NINE
The Long Road Home

Michael heard Jessica, Hope and Kelsey talking quietly in the kitchen when he exited Jessica's room. He was not sure whether or not to bring up what his father had discussed in their phone conversation. Watching the women sitting around the table talking quietly, he decided against it. There was plenty of time for him to mention it later on. He headed into the living room unnoticed and clicked on the television. He leaned back and then realized he should send something to Anna who was still in the dark. He sent her a quick text, letting her know there had been some serious complications and to pray; he would contact her with more details when he was able. She immediately responded letting him know that she would pray and would have her family pray as well. He thought briefly of the dance, but then put that idea out of his head.

Kelsey rounded the corner and came to sit on the sofa by Michael.

She turned her attention to the television and began braiding her long, black hair over her shoulder.

"I think I would like to go to confession," she told him quietly when a commercial come on.

He nodded his head.

"I can make a call and set it up for this afternoon. That work for you?"

"As long as you can drive me," she agreed.

Michael flipped open his phone and called Fr. Gregory Mary to arrange their confession times. As he did, Kelsey left the room and went back into the bedroom she was using. Michael hung up from his call and returned his attention to the television. He was hoping to spend some time in pursuit of sheer meaninglessness. He flipped off his shoes and swung his legs up onto the couch.

Hope was shaking Michael gently awake.

"Hey there," she said quietly.

"Did I fall asleep?" he asked sheepishly.

"I think you're entitled," Hope told him.

"What's Kelsey up to?" He sat up on the sofa and rubbed a hand over his eyes.

"It's about time for you two to leave for your appointment with Fr. Gregory Mary," she told him.

"How did you know?" he asked.

"Kelsey told us," she responded smiling.

He nodded his head.

"Hope," he said quietly, "would you please continue to pray about this situation with Kelsey? I'm concerned there's more going on than meets the eye."

Hope looked at him questioningly but nodded her head emphatically. "Of course."

Michael headed into the bathroom to freshen up. He went into the office and changed into a pair of khaki pants and navy polo shirt. When he came out, Kelsey was leaning against the counter in the kitchen, waiting for him to be ready. She had changed again as well. This time she was wearing a pair of black jeans and a gray turtleneck sweater. Her black hair hung in a long braid down her back and though she was still pale, her complexion had evened out since she had stopped crying. He had never seen her out of the over-size black hoodie. This girl was a bit closer to the one that he remembered from High School. She smiled shyly as he realized he had been studying her intently.

"Oh— I'll be right there," he said, going back to the office quickly to get his prayer book.

As he walked with Kelsey to the back door he called over his shoulder, "Anyone need anything?"

"Nope!" Jessica called from the basement.

"Hope went back home," Kelsey told him as she walked out the back door that he was holding for her.

The two left and drove the short distance to St. Paul's parish. Michael turned on some soft music. Kelsey didn't speak, but he could see that she was wringing her hands silently in her lap. He pulled the car up to a stop in a parking spot next to the back door of the rectory. They got out of the car at the same time and Michael stepped back to allow Kelsey to walk in front of him.

"It'll be fine, Kels," he assured her as he touched her shoulder gently.

Fr. Gregory Mary answered their knock. He was a tall man, a few inches taller even than Michael. He had a full beard the same dark color as his short brown hair. He offered his hand first to Kelsey as she entered and then to Michael who came in behind her. He noticed Kelsey's hand shaking slightly when they shook.

"Welcome," he said genially. He motioned for them to sit on the small bench in the foyer. "Can I bring you something to drink? Water? Soda?"

"No thank you," Michael said.

"Water," Kelsey said in a sound that came out more like a squeak. She cleared her throat.

"Water, please," she said again.

"Whoever would like to go first can proceed into my study," Father said motioning to a door which was left ajar. He turned and walked back down a short hallway. Kelsey could hear him opening the refrigerator.

"Do you want to go first?" Michael asked.

She shook her head quickly so Michael stood and walked toward the study. He stopped and turned retracing his steps. He handed Kelsey his prayer book and a small brochure about going to confession, as Fr. Gregory Mary returned with a small water bottle.

Father gave Michael a moment to settle himself in the study.

"We'll be just a few minutes," Father said to Kelsey who nodded and took a drink from the water bottle.

After some time, Michael came out and Kelsey stood up quickly. He patted her shoulder as she passed him and entered the brightly paneled room. She turned and shut the door quietly behind her.

"Hello Kelsey," Fr. Gregory Mary said gently. He was standing behind his desk, near the door. "It is so good to have you here."

Kelsey smiled uncertainly.

"We will meet here, toward the back of the room," Father motioned with his hand toward two chairs. She passed in front of him.

"And I will leave this door a bit ajar trusting that Michael will not listen in." He opened the door once more and pushed it open about six inches, concerned about her comfort in being alone in a room with him.

Kelsey looked from Father, through the crack in the door, to where she could see Michael who smiled from over on the bench. He had plugged his ears good-naturedly. She turned back to Father who gave her a friendly laugh.

"Unless you are comfortable with me closing it altogether," he added.

Kelsey smiled. "That would be fine. It's been so long Father, since I've been to confession, if we leave the door open, Michael might have heart failure."

Everyone laughed and Kelsey passed easily over to the chair.

Michael bowed his head to say a quick prayer of Thanksgiving. Jessica was right; Fr. Gregory Mary was certainly a gem. It was a gift for Kelsey to have found him. He flipped open his phone and started to play a game to pass the time. He thought again about Anna and the dance. He felt foolish obsessing on this issue. He switched over to texting.

- How are things going with the dance?

He read the lines once, twice and then just clicked the send button. He had no idea what Anna's schedule was for the day. Perhaps, if she was at work, it would be hours before he heard from her. His phone buzzed immediately. She had responded.

- I've asked Hope to go with me and Mom to find a dress.
- So you're going then?
- Well, maybe.

Michael shook his head exasperatedly. What the heck did that mean? Before he had a chance to respond another text came in.

- How are things going over there?
- Better now; Kelsey is in confession.
- Awesome. U r a great friend.
- Can I call you later?

Michael suddenly had this strange feeling — like something had shifted in the way he communicated with Anna. He had never before asked permission to call her.

- I would like that.

He smiled widely as the door to the study opened and Kelsey came out. Her eyes were puffy from crying, but she looked more serene than he had seen her. She smiled at him as he stood up.

"Can we go to the church to do our penance?" she asked Fr. Gregory Mary, looking over her shoulder.

"Of course," the priest replied, "and I hope you will consider staying for Mass as well. It will be beginning at 5:30."

Kelsey looked at Michael questioningly. "Can we stay?"

"Sure," Michael responded, turning to grasp the door handle to hide his wide smile.

Fr. Gregory Mary followed them to the front door and gave them a quick blessing before letting them go.

To Kelsey he said, "You have my number; please call me at any time."

"Thank you, Father."

Michael and Kelsey crossed the parking lot and climbed the stone steps to the front of the church. A few people had already begun to arrive. Michael turned his phone on silent before entering and Kelsey did the same thing. They walked through the heavy wooden doors and into a beautifully decorated church. They tread silently up the carpeted aisle toward the handsomely engraved gold tabernacle. Both of them knelt in the front pew to say their penance prayers and meditate before Mass began.

At the end of the homily, Fr. Gregory Mary made a short announcement. "Though there seems to be some confusion these days over who should present oneself for communion, I would like to remind all of you that the teaching of the

Catechism is clear: those Catholics not in grave mortal sin are invited to present themselves for communion. Everyone else is invited to present themselves for a blessing and join us by offering a Spiritual Communion. The Spiritual Communion prayer can be found on the back page of your missal."

Kelsey and Michael shared a smile as Fr. Gregory Mary continued on with the celebration of the Mass without missing a beat. Truly, they had found a man of God in this parish and they were both grateful.

Michael and Kelsey followed the rest of the parishioners out of the beautiful church. They stood toward the back, waiting until Father was free. They took turns shaking his hand and thanking him for a truly spiritual afternoon. They drove the short distance back to Jessica's house in silence. This time however, the silence was serene and not tension-filled.

"Thank you Michael," Kelsey said as Michael turned into the drive.

"Don't thank me;" Michael told her, "I was just the instrument."

Jessica was bustling around the kitchen finishing up dinner when the two came in the back door.

"What's with the spread?" Michael asked, shrugging out of his coat and hanging it on the back of the chair.

"Put that in your room," Kelsey told him, "Can't you see you are spoiling the effect?"

Hope laughed as she finished pouring water into the goblets.

Michael drifted past her with his coat. "Smells yummy!"

"Chicken piccata," Jessica told them. "We worry about how well you college kids eat when you are away."

In another moment, the four of them were sitting around the table talking and laughing and enjoying their Saturday night. It was nice to put away all the fear and anguish for a short time and just hang out. It was hard to believe that things had changed so dramatically since the morning. Often times during the meal, Kelsey would be silent, lost in thought, but after a few moments, she would laugh at some silly story Michael was sharing.

Kelsey and Michael insisted on clearing the table at the end of the meal while Jessica and Hope remained at the table drinking tea.

"Should we rent a movie?" Hope asked everyone.

"You guys can go ahead," Kelsey told them. "I'm just going to change into my jammies, lie in bed and read a book."

Michael nodded his head in agreement. "No offense ladies, but I'm pretty worn out myself."

"Hope, we're putting these college folks to shame," Jessica pointed out and the two women laughed easily.

"Go watch your movie!" Michael exclaimed, as they both got up and headed into the front room.

Michael dried the last plate and put it away while Kelsey washed her hands.

"Are you really okay?" he asked softly, putting his hand on her shoulder.

Kelsey nodded her head. Laughter from the living room drifted into the kitchen. She hung the dishtowel over the side of the sink.

"I'm really doing okay right now," she assured him, looking back over her shoulder. "I just want to decompress a bit."

He nodded his head in agreement and put his arms around her, resting his chin on her shoulder. "I'm proud of you, Kels."

She smiled but did not respond. He let her go and backed up a couple of steps so she could leave the kitchen.

Poking her head into the front room, she waved at Hope

and Jessica.

"We'll try to keep it down out here," Jessica teased, "to let you young-uns get some sleep."

Michael laughed as he followed Kelsey down the narrow hall.

"Sleep well, Kels," he told her.

She looked at him ruefully. She hadn't said it aloud, but she was concerned with what kind of demons sleep would bring. "You too."

Michael was back in the office, sitting on the desk chair with his heart pounding loudly as he looked at his cell phone and considered calling Anna.

Don't be ridiculous, he thought. *You talk to Anna all the time.*

Anna picked up on the first ring. "Hey," she said.
"Hi Anna."

"What's going on over there; is everything okay?" she asked impatiently.

Michael tried to give her the condensed version of the day's events regarding Kelsey and the baby. As he was speaking, he realized that it had not even been a full day since the news. So much had happened since he woke this morning. He suddenly felt overwhelmed and he sighed aloud.

"You sound tired," Anna observed.

"Yeah," he admitted, "I am. It's been a crazy day."

"I can understand that."

"And I didn't even tell you the whole other part of it," Michael said.

"There's more?"

"So then I spoke to my father this afternoon also," he explained, "Do you remember what I had said to you about the clusters of pregnancies?"

"Yeah," Anna said.

"Well, the vast majority of those are resulting in major complications — like end of life for the baby — complications," he said.

"And you think Kelsey is involved in this trend?" Anna asked concerned.

"Yeah, I do," he said warily.

"Have you spoken to her about it?"

"No," he replied.

"I don't think you should," Anna said quickly. "I think you should just let it go and wait to see what the doctor finds out. It won't help Kelsey to feel any better by knowing now. You can always tell her later."

"I agree," Michael said.

"Wow Michael, that's kinda crazy," Anna said after a few minutes.

"Enough about all that," Michael said brightening. "Tell me what's going on with the dance."

"Well, I talked to my mother about it and she thinks that Dad will let me go. Actually, I think that she is going to discuss it with him first and then we are all going to talk about it."

"That's cool," Michael remarked.

"But I don't think I'm going to go with a date," she confessed.

"How come?" His stomach was suddenly in a knot.

"Too complicated," she said. "And besides, there just isn't anyone at school I would even consider going with."

"Would you consider going with me?" he blurted out. "You know, as friends?"

Anna laughed nervously. "That's really nice of you, Michael, but I wouldn't make you suffer through something like that... especially with a group of people that you don't even know."

"Well, I know you," he told her. "And I wouldn't categorize

spending an evening in your company as any sort of suffering."

Anna was silent for a moment and Michael cleared his throat nervously.

"I would really like that," Anna said quietly, "as long as you promise that you aren't feeling obligated to do this. I mean I really can go on my own."

"Seriously, Anna," he assured her, "I'm not feeling obligated at all. I would be honored if you would allow me to escort you to the dance. I will call your father this evening to get his permission."

"Thank you Michael, that would be very kind," she told him.

They talked for a few more minutes about the details of the event and then they ended the call.

Michael sat in the desk chair and looked at the picture on Jessica's office wall. It was a group shot from last summer. All of the families together for a picnic before he and some others left for their first year of college. Michael laughed aloud. That was the party where he realized that Anna was now a young women, not a little kid any more. They had talked together almost the entire afternoon. Remembering made him smile. He glanced at the clock. It was still early enough.

Michael had to face the daunting task of calling Timothy and it unsettled him a bit. It wasn't that he was afraid of Timothy, he was more afraid that Timothy would pick up on the fact that he liked Anna as much more than a friend.

He took a deep breath and called Anna's house number.

Jane answered the phone and called loudly to her father.

"Dad! It's Michael on the phone!"

No chance of discretion from this point on, Michael knew.

"Hey Michael," Timothy said picking up the call from another room.

Michael waited a moment to hear the click of the other line.

"Hi Tim, how are you?" Michael asked.

"I'm great. So what's going on over there? Anna tells us that there have been some serious complications."

"Yes, there have been. I don't have many details at this point, but thank you for your prayers," Michael told him. "And that really isn't the reason for my call."

"Oh?" Timothy asked. "Okay then, What's up?"

"Well, I called because I wanted to ask for your permission to take Anna to her winter formal," Michael said quickly, "You know, as friends."

Timothy paused for a half second. "Well, that's really very thoughtful of you, Michael," he said. "I'll need to discuss it with Lily."

"Of course," Michael said.

"Have you spoken to Anna about this already?" Timothy asked.

"Yes, I have," Michael told him, "We just spoke about it this evening and I told her I would be calling you tonight as well."

"Okay, that's fine. Thank you for calling me so quickly," Timothy told him, "Let me speak to Lily about it this evening and I will call you back tomorrow. Is that okay?"

"Sure, that's great," Michael agreed.

"Thanks for calling Michael," Timothy said.

"Sure thing. I'll talk to you tomorrow," Michael said.

"Have a good night," Timothy said. "Say hi to everyone for us."

"Will do; you too."

Michael hung up the phone and took a deep breath. He looked toward the door. He thought about going to tell Jessica and Hope, but then he was not sure what Timothy and Lily would decide. He changed into pajamas and lay back on his cot. He thought about the different things that Timothy and Lilly could be discussing right then and he fell asleep thinking about spending a fun night in Anna's company.

When Michael woke up the next morning, the house was completely silent. He padded into the kitchen. The clock said 11:00. There was a note on the table that just said "Church". The coffee maker was still plugged in and turned on so he poured himself a cup of coffee and tried to think about how to best organize his day. He sat at the table scratching at the stubble on his chin. He hadn't shaved in two days. He looked out into the back yard and thought about what needed doing. First, he needed to bring Kelsey back to his place to get her car. He felt she should do this sooner rather than later because one – she had a long drive ahead of her and two — he still felt she should stop to speak to her parents. The sooner she was able to get back, the sooner she would have some real information about Adam as well.

Michael knew that situation with Adam was weighing heavily on Kelsey, along with everything else she was facing. He knew that she felt somehow responsible for Adam's poor judgment — if that is what it was. Taking his coffee with him, he headed into the bathroom for a quick shower. He hoped that by the time he was ready, Jessica and Hope would be back and Kelsey would be awake.

Michael was just bringing his bag out to his car, when Jessica pulled into the driveway.

"Hey there," Michael said as Jessica, Hope and Kelsey got out of the car.

"Hey," everyone chorused back.

"Kels, I wanted to talk to you about the plan for today," Michael said laughing. "I thought you were still asleep."

Kelsey hung back while Hope and Jessica went into the

house talking about Martha's return from vacation.

"Well, Hope and Jessica have various activities including picking up all of the kids this afternoon, and I really should get back pretty quickly. I'd like to see if I can get more information on Adam," Kelsey explained.

Michael was nodding. "I've already packed up my stuff so we can leave here whenever you're ready." He shut the hatchback of his car.

"Everything of mine is all set in Stevie's room," she told him.

"Great, then I'll get it now and we can say our goodbyes," he told her. They both turned and walked toward the house.

Michael passed through the kitchen and off into Stevie's room to get Kelsey's overnight bag. When he came back around the corner, there were hugs and tears happening in the kitchen.

"We'll keep praying for you," Hope was saying.

"And you can call any time," Jessica was saying.

"I know; thank you both so much," Kelsey was saying.

"Okay, break it up — break it up!" Michael said, "What about me?"

"You are just a goof!" Hope told him, coming to give him a big hug.

"But we love you anyway," Jessica said, taking her turn to give him a hug and then a shot in the ribs. "And don't be such a stranger this time. We never see you unless there's some kind of crisis going on!"

Michael bowed his head sheepishly; that was mainly true.

"Get out of here, you two," Hope said, "Drive safe and keep in touch. You too, Kelsey!"

Everyone waved as they headed out the door.

Michael threw Kelsey's bag into the back of his car and opened her door. She looked back at the house for a long while as they drove away.

"You have amazing friends," Kelsey said again as he steered the car up onto the highway.

He nodded in agreement. "Yeah," he said, "God has blessed me that way."

After a few minutes, he glanced at Kelsey who was just sitting quietly fingering a Rosary bracelet that one of the women must have given her.

"Are you going to stop at your parents?"

She sighed. "I don't think so."

"Why not?" he pressed.

"We haven't had the best of relationships lately," she answered. "I know that I need to talk to them and I know we have a lot to work out. I'd just like to have more answers from the doctor before I get into it with them."

Michael nodded. "I don't know if I agree with your strategy, but I understand what you are saying," he told her.

"Instead, I'm going to see if I can't get in touch with McKenna and track down what in the world is going on with Adam," she said, pushing her dark hair back over her ear. "I think that situation is more important to take care of right now."

"What are you going to do?" he asked.

"Well, that depends on how things are going with him," she said. "Obviously, I'm going to tell him there's no baby. I'm just not sure how I'm going to handle the breaking up part."

Michael nodded. It seemed that Kelsey was ready to make some tough decisions to try to get her life back on track.

"And I should probably find a hair dresser," she murmured, pointing a lock of hair in his direction.

"Don't you like the black?" Michael asked her confused.

"Not so much, no."

They laughed together and talked of other things on their ride back to Michael's apartment.

Michael pulled his car into the spot right next to Kelsey's and popped the latch on his hatchback. He went around to open her door and then pulled up the hatch and retrieved her bag from inside.

Michael threw Kelsey's bag into her backseat once her car was unlocked. He stopped the door when she opened it and pulled her into a tight hug instead.

She buried her head in his shoulder and cried.

"Hey," he said gently, "You're okay. You don't have to cry."

"I'm just so grateful to you, Michael," she told him, "I have never had anyone care so much about me like you and your friends did."

"But your family ... " he protested.

"They don't even know who I am anymore," she said. She pulled back slightly and looked up into Michael's face.

"How can I ever thank you?" she asked him.

He met her gaze and held it for a few moments. Her large hazel eyes glimmered with tears.

"Just think Kelsey, think! And know that you are a beautiful woman that God made special. Don't give yourself away foolishly and don't change who you are for someone else."

She bowed her head back into his chest and hugged him tighter.

He kissed the top of her head before pushing her gently away. "And I will be your friend no matter what," he assured her, his blue eyes twinkling

"I'm afraid of what's to come," she said honestly. "Afraid of what the doctor has to say..."

"But you won't have to go through that alone. We will be here for you," he insisted.

She nodded her head. "Does this mean I don't have to call in every day now?"

"You can call as often as you like," he told her smiling. She smiled too.

"Have you told Anna?" she asked.

He nodded his head. "She's praying for you."

Kelsey nodded. "Tell her thank you from me."

"Tell her yourself, and be careful driving," he told her as he opened her car door.

She got in and rolled down the window.

"I love you, Michael," she said. "You know ..."

"as a brother," they said together.

"I know Kels, and I love you too."

He watched her drive away and said a prayer of Thanksgiving for all of the good that God had brought out of a very difficult situation.

......................•●•....................

Michael's cell phone rang as he was unpacking his duffle bag in his bedroom. It was Timothy. Michael noticed the time was one-thirty when he answered it.

"Hello," Michael said, trying not to sound nervous.

"Hey Michael. It's Tim."

"Hey Tim, how are you?" Michael asked, leaning up against his desk.

"I'm great, yourself?" Timothy asked.

"Actually, really good," Michael said. "Kelsey has left and I believe that she has made some good decisions about beginning to deal with her situation."

"That's great," Timothy said, "I'm calling to see if you are free to come over for dinner. Lily and I would like some time to speak with you and Anna."

"Uh, of course," Michael replied, rubbing his free hand on his thigh.

"It's no big deal," Timothy assured him, "We'd just like to talk to the two of you."

"Um, okay," Michael answered, "What time?"

"We'll eat at five, but you can come over any time."

"That's great, I'll see you soon then," Michael told him.

"See you later," Timothy said.

Michael flipped his phone shut and finished unpacking. His roommates were still out so he had the place to himself. He grabbed his philosophy reading and went to sit on the sofa. He wanted to see if he could read the assignment before dinner.

Dinner... He felt a bit nervous by the prospect. He did not want there to be any real shift in the relationship he had with Anna. It was true that he liked her but he also knew they were both young and it would be many years before they could speak seriously about marriage. He just hoped to be able to take her to the dance and spend some time with her socially. And he didn't want everyone to make a big deal about it.

Michael plowed through a couple of chapters of philosophy before he needed to get ready to go back to Hadley. So much for saving on gas these days! He considered the prospect of changing his clothes. He wanted Timothy and Lily to know that he took this meeting seriously but also that he was not attempting to overly impress them. He decided to change out of a t-shirt into a long-sleeve polo. That seemed a good compromise.

Traffic was light and Michael was able to get to Hadley in a half hour. He pulled to a stop on the street in front of the Warner house. As soon as he opened the door, Lucy came running around the side yard to see him, her pony-tail bobbing wildly.

"Hi Michael," she called with glee.

Michael waved and bent down to sweep her up into a big hug. "Long time no see."

"I missed you," she told him, squeezing him tight around his neck.

"I missed you too," he said, kissing the top of her head.
"Are you coming for dinner?"

"Want a piggy back?" he asked instead.

Lucy squealed with delight and Michael shifted her around to his back. "Hold on tight," he told her.

Michael started walking to the front door.

"They're in the back!" Lucy squealed, laughing at him.

He turned with a smile and started walking down the side yard, bouncing Lucy on his back. Timothy and the rest of the clan were in back raking. Michael crouched down so Lucy could slide off and then he went over and took the rake from Lily.

"Let me do that," he told her. Over his shoulder he said, "Hey, Anna. Hi Everyone."

Lily smiled and passed him the rake. Michael was a handsome young man. He looked nice in his long-sleeve polo and jeans. She could see why Anna would be eager to go with him to the dance.

"Hi Michael," Anna said shyly, meeting his blue eyes with her deep brown ones.

Instantly the color rose to his cheeks and he had to look away.

Lily smiled knowingly and called all of the girls into the house, leaving the guys out to clear up the small section of yard that was left.

"Hey Michael," Zack said smiling and swinging his rake like a weapon.

"How did tryouts go?" Michael asked, blocking the rake dramatically and flicking Zack's baseball cap off his head at the same time.

Zack laughed then asked, "How did you know?"
He let the rake fall to the ground, bent to grab his ball cap and looked at his father suspiciously.

"I spent the weekend at Jessica's," Michael answered.

"It's like having three mothers!" Zack complained good-naturedly, putting the cap back onto his head and picking up the rake.

They all laughed.

"It's good to see you, Michael," Timothy said, clapping him on the back.

"Yeah, you too."

"Can you two finish up this small patch and I'll start the grill?" Timothy asked. "I don't think there will be that many grilling days left."

Zack and Michael nodded.

Timothy went up the steps to the grill which was sitting on the deck. He leaned the rake against the side of the house, lit the propane and then disappeared into the house. He returned a short time later with a plate heaping with burgers, hot dogs and chicken.

"Looks like a feast," Michael said.

"Sundays rock," Zack said simply.

Michael laughed as he leaned over to pick up the last few piles of leaves with his rake. By the time the guys could smell the food cooking on the grill, they had filled the last bag with leaves and set upon the task of dragging all the bags to the front curb for pick up. Zack and Michael went in the front door and had just finished washing in the small bathroom when Timothy came in the back with all the food.

Everyone found a spot at the table — Michael had to sit next to Lucy. Timothy said grace and then they all started passing plates, talking and laughing at once. Zack was recounting his audition story for Michael. Jane and Lucy were talking about a school activity they had planned for the next week. Anna and her father were discussing the legislation that had been proposed which would raise the minimum wage and why so many politicians did not support it. Lily watched everyone silently, a contented smile on her face.

"What's for dessert?" Lucy demanded when she had eaten the last bite of her hot dog.

"There's ice cream," Lily told her. "But only if you mind your manners."

"Hurray! Ice cream, please."

"We are going to wait for a little while before we have dessert," Timothy explained to her.

"Okay," Lucy agreed.

Jane and Anna started clearing the plates.

"Zack, would you please clear?" Timothy asked standing up and stretching his back.

"But I cleared last night," Zack protested loudly.

"Your mom and I need to talk to Anna and Michael," Timothy explained.

"Why does she always get out of her chores?" Zack asked.

"Zachariah," Lily said in the mother tone of voice.

Zack pushed back his chair in defeat and began helping his younger sister with the table.

Anna and Michael followed Timothy and Lily into the dining room. "You can put on a movie downstairs when you are finished," Lily said to the kitchen crew in passing.

Timothy sat at the head of the table and motioned for Michael to sit to his right. Lily and Anna both went around to the other side of the table.

"Do you want coffee or tea?" Lily asked Michael, smiling kindly as Anna took a seat.

"Yeah, coffee would be great," he said trying not to sound nervous. He could tell Lily was trying to stall until the kids had finished up in the kitchen. He was grateful.

Lily returned to the kitchen and bustled around a bit with the coffee. She hurried the others up and sent them down to the basement. When she returned with a mug of coffee for Timothy and a mug for Michael, the basement door was just closing.

"Michael and Anna," Timothy began, "Your mother and I talked about the Winter formal last night and we want you to know that it would be fine for the two of you to attend together."

Michael nodded and Anna smiled shyly, pushing her dark wavy hair to the side.

"There are a couple of things we'd like to ask however," he went on.

Anna looked pointedly at her father. She fidgeted, smoothing down the sleeves of her green cardigan, knowing that the next words out of his mouth were going to embarrass her.

"First off, Michael, I will be driving you to and from the dance," Timothy said.

Anna opened her mouth to protest.

"Sure, that's fine," Michael cut her off.

"We trust you, Michael," Lily said, pushing a curl of her dark hair behind her ear and leaning in his direction.

"I know you do," Michael told her.

"We just don't feel it would be a good situation for you two to have access to a car in case you would like to leave the event early. We would prefer to know where you are," Lily finished.

"Mom…" Anna began.

"Of course," Michael interrupted.

"You could call us if you wanted to leave," Timothy told them. "And we want you to know that we have already decided no after-party activities for this one."

"The prom is different," Lily explained, "because there is an after-party already organized at the school."

"I had one of those," Michael told her.

"How was it?"

"Pretty fun actually," he answered.

Michael saw Anna watching him speaking with her mother. She was frowning slightly and he felt bad, like she saw him taking her parents' side in this.

"There is nothing officially organized after this dance and we don't want the two of you going off to hang out at someone's house," Timothy said.

"Dad..." Anna began.

"These are the rules," Timothy told her.

Anna sat back in her chair, crossing her arms silently. Michael could sense that she felt her parents were being unfair. He would have felt the same way at one time, but now he understood all the more the importance of a father's need to keep his daughter safe.

"You are welcome to come back here and watch a movie or something," Lily offered.

The room was silent for a few moments.

"Well, that's all we got," Timothy said smiling. "Is that acceptable?"

Anna leaned forward. Michael remained silent, waiting for her to speak.

"It's fine," she said finally. She glanced over at Michael. "But are you sure he can't drive?"

"I'm afraid not," Timothy said again.

Anna frowned and looked to Michael.

He smiled easily. "It all sounds great to me! What time do I pick you up? Uh, I mean, meet you here?"

Michael, Timothy and Lily laughed. Anna rolled her eyes.

"We'll let you two discuss some of the other details," Timothy said, as he and Lily stood together and left the dining room.

Anna and Michael sat awkwardly in silence for a few moments. Michael felt badly for her — he had absolutely no issue with the rules for the night, but he knew that she felt her parents did not trust her. He wanted to say something, but he was afraid of saying the wrong thing. He looked over at her. She was wearing a green cardigan over a black tee and jeans. She looked comfortable but dismayed at her parents' lack of tact. He smiled at her encouragingly.

"I'm sorry about all that," Anna said finally, clasping her hands on the table and looking down. "I'm afraid they've gotten a bit carried away. Seriously — it's just a dance."

Michael leaned on the table toward her. He reached for her hand and then thought better of it. He placed his hands palm down on the table in front of him. "Anna, I don't feel the least bit put upon by your parents' requests."

She looked up at him. "Really?"

"Yes, really."

"You should at least be able to drive," she protested.

"Really, it's no big deal," he told her. "So, tell me the rest of the details. What color is your dress? Have you found one yet?"

She smiled broadly and Michael smiled with her. Rules or not, it would be a great night.

CHAPTER TEN
Schism

 ichael walked out of church and stood outside to greet the priest at the parish he had attended Sunday Mass at since arriving at college. Fr.

Richard was smiling and shaking hands with his parishioners. He was blessing babies and throwing fists with young boys. The priest was a stocky middle-aged man, balding at the crown. Michael stood to the side and watched the scene unfold. He thought Fr. Richard was a great priest and he hoped to get a few minutes to speak to him alone.

After the last stragglers headed toward the parking lot, Fr. Richard turned his attention to Michael who was still leaning against the brick of the building.

"Hey there," Fr. Richard said pleasantly, walking over to Michael and offering his hand.

"Hi Father. How are you?" Michael asked, shaking hands firmly.

"I'm doing well, Michael. I heard from Fr. Oscar that you gave an amazing talk at his youth group event last week," Fr. Richard said. "Do you have time for a coffee this morning?"

"Sure," Michael told him.

"Let me go to the sacristy and get out of these vestments

and then we can head over to the diner for a quick cup o' joe."

Michael followed Fr. Richard back into the church. He knelt in silent prayer in the first pew while Father went into the back, where the sacristy was located. In a few moments, Father came back into the sanctuary and knelt to the side of the altar to say his mid-day office. When he had finished praying, Fr. Richard stood up and walked back down to where Michael was now sitting. Standing quickly, Michael followed Father out the side door of the Church and over to his car which was parked next to the rectory. They drove the five minutes to the diner in quiet contemplation.

"Just two coffees please," Fr. Richard told the waitress behind the counter as he and Michael perched upon two round stools.

"Sure thing, Father," the waitress replied smiling pleasantly.

"I'm guessing you heard what's been going on at St. Monica's," Michael began after a long moment. "What do you think of it? And why didn't you say anything about receiving communion?"

The waitress placed two steaming mugs of coffee before the two men and a small bowl filled with plastic creamers. The men murmured their thanks.

"What is there to say?" Fr. Richard asked, swiveling the stool to face Michael.

"How about — what's happening at St. Monica's is wrong and you shouldn't go to communion if you aren't Catholic?" Michael asked, gesturing angrily with his full plastic creamer.

"Michael, for years and years, people have been coming to communion who shouldn't be. Nothing about this is new," Fr. Richard told him calmly, trying not to let his smile betray him. He didn't want Michael to think that he wasn't taking him seriously; it was just that the vigor of youth amused him.

"Except now the Pastor at St. Monica's wants to welcome it," Michael complained, "on purpose!"

"I heard from Fr. Oscar that you spoke about some of that when you talked to his youth group kids."

"Some of them had questions," Michael defended.

"And what did you say?" Father asked.

"I explained that it was the responsibility of the person who was receiving communion first and foremost, but that still doesn't excuse public scandal," Michael replied heatedly.

"What do you think should be done?" Fr. Richard asked, stirring his coffee.

"I think that all priests around here should remind their parishioners of what it says in the Catechism. In that way you wouldn't be denying people communion but you would be placing some of the responsibility with them, where it belongs."

"That seems a fair assessment," Father replied.

"Why would any pastor choose to do this anyway?" Michael asked.

"I believe it's a misguided sense of unity," Fr. Richard told him.

Michael shook his head, taking a drink of coffee.

"I don't think, in the end, that the Bishop will stand for it," Fr. Richard said.

"And what's taking him so long to respond?" Michael asked.

"It has only been a couple of weeks now, Michael. I would imagine the Bishop has been in consultation with many people over that time. These things take time, patience and great pastoral attention," Father replied.

"And in the meantime, everything is being all messed up over here," Michael complained.

Father Richard smiled widely, "I don't know that I would say that."

"How can you not?"

"You aren't the first person who has come to me with the idea of teaching from the Catechism, Michael," Fr. Richard explained, "One thing that has come from this bump in the road is that I have heard many more people around here — folks I only see at Sunday Mass — speaking about communion. What it is; who should receive it."

"Really?" Michael asked in surprise.

"Yes, really," Fr. Richard told him. "I even got a couple of phone calls at the rectory last week."

"I guess that's a good thing," Michael said.

"It's the kind of thing that makes a people stop and assess what they are really doing at Mass."

"What do you think will end up happening in the end, Father?" Michael asked.

"I believe that there will be priests who move away from Rome," Father said sadly, "That is usually the way these things end."

Michael pondered this thought and then nodded slowly.

"This has essentially been going on for years, Michael. Things like this have occurred since the foundation of our Church. History calls them heresies," Father told him. "It just so happens that right now it's occurring in our backyard. I'm not sure how this division is going to affect the Catholic faithful in our area."

"Perhaps this is the gift that the progressives of the Church in our area have been looking for," Michael suggested, "and this is the beginning of a faction of American Catholics that will openly ordain women, support birth control... you know, all that stuff that's been hanging around on the periphery of the Church here since the late 60's and early 70's."

Fr. Richard was nodding his head solemnly. "There are many who want the church to go in that direction, priests and nuns included. I still believe that they are all operating from a misguided sense of unity."

"I think you are too kind," Michael answered sharply.

"Judge not, lest ye be judged... Charity at all times, Michael," Father reminded him.

Michael scowled but did not reply.

"And what will you do about all this?" Fr. Richard asked, after a few minutes of reflection.

"I will continue to speak out where I'm able. I really believe that the new translation of the Catechism was a gift to the Church. We need it to be able to speak to this new tangential split," Michael explained.

"You're a smart young man," Fr. Richard said, setting down his empty cup and looking at the clock on the wall. The diner was beginning to get busier.

"Have you considered becoming a priest?"

Michael laughed good-naturedly.

"It's really not my vocation. I go to school with seminarians remember — I've been down that road before."

Fr. Richard laughed as well.

"You can't blame a guy for trying."

Father drove the few minutes back to the parish parking lot where Michael had left his car. They spoke of sports and the annual parish fair, which was currently being planned. The two men got out at the same time. Fr. Richard circled around and gave Michael a hearty hug. Father walked with him to the car. Before sending him on his way, Fr. Richard gave Michael a blessing

When Michael returned to his apartment, he headed into his room to change into jeans and a tee-shirt. He grabbed his cell phone and gave a quick call over to the Warner house.

"Hey Zack, I'm looking for your dad," Michael said.

A moment later, Timothy picked up the extension in

his home office where he was reviewing a paper that Zack had written for history.

"Hey there," Timothy said, leaning back in his chair and putting the paper aside.

"Hello," Michael replied.

"What can I do for you on this fine Sunday?" Timothy asked, crossing his legs at the ankle.

"I've been praying for you all," Michael told him. "I just wanted to check in on how things are going over where you are."

"Well, if you're asking me about the communion issue, the priests that I have spoken to have all taken to citing catechism entries about worthily receiving before the distribution of communion," Timothy told him.

Michael smiled and walked out of his room to find something to drink. "Is it a movement?"

Timothy laughed. "Perhaps it is. How are things where you are?"

"Well," Michael replied, pouring a glass of milk, "I had an interesting conversation with Fr. Richard after Mass this morning. In the end, he doesn't think the Bishop will stand for it."

"There seems to be a consensus on that here as well," Timothy told him.

"How are you handling things?" Michael asked.

Timothy was moved to hear the sincere concern in Michael's voice.

"Well, I'm finding opportunities to talk about communion when I can," Timothy replied. "I still haven't taken my family back to the parish. I'm really praying about what God is asking me to do in my position."

"Yeah, Fr. Richard said he heard a lot of talk about communion as well," Michael said. "I'm so sorry that this is having such an impact on your job as well as your family, Tim. What do you think will happen in the end?"

"Well, they'll either replace the pastor fairly quickly or I think there will be some kind of confrontation," Timothy told him. "In practical circumstance, people that agree with the new Pastor's theology are beginning to travel to his parish."

"Yeah, Father Richard and I were discussing the same thing," Michael agreed, placing his empty glass in the sink. "That could be messy."

"We just have to keep up the prayers and do what we can to support the priests who are speaking the truth," Timothy told him, climbing the stairs to the family room.

"I agree," Michael said. "I just can't really believe it's happening here."

"Are you watching the game today?" Timothy asked, settling onto the sofa and clicking on the television.

"I wish," Michael replied, turning the corner back into his bedroom. "Duty calls. I've got a paper due at the end of the week."

"Well, stick with it," Timothy told him, sounding like the father he is.

"Yeah, yeah," Michael said, chuckling, and lowering himself into his desk chair.

"I'll catch up with you soon. We'll have you over for dinner," Timothy said.

"Sounds great," Michael agreed, opening his laptop. "See ya."

"Yeah, bye."

Michael worked for about a half-hour on the outline for his paper and then decided he should head to the library to get started on his research. At about five-thirty, he decided to take a break. He returned to the apartment to have some dinner.

Michael piled his laptop, book bag and one stray library

book onto the kitchen table. He went over to the fridge and opened it. It was apparent that three men lived in the house. The fridge was empty except for a half-gallon of milk, three cans of beer for Michael's roommates and two old pizza boxes on the bottom shelf.

Surveying the barren fridge, Michael decided on peanut butter and jelly. He pulled the grape jelly from the fridge door, retrieved the peanut butter from the cabinet and found a loaf of bread on the counter under yesterday's mail. He brought everything to the kitchen table. Opening his laptop, he quickly made two sandwiches and waited for his laptop to load. For the next few minutes, he spent some time surfing the Internet looking for stories about issues of distribution of communion. Father Richard was right; this type of thing had happened before and was happening all around them. According to his research, it took some time for things like this to get sorted out. One of Michael's friends, a local Catholic Blogger, had been talking at length about the issue both here and in the general area. Michael checked the website for the diocese and there was still no official statement. He clicked away from the page in disappointment. He finished his second sandwich and closed his laptop. After quickly cleaning up his dinner things, he headed to the sofa to watch some TV.

At seven that evening, Michael received a text from Jessica.

- The pope has called a couple of Bishops in our area to Rome.
- How do you know?
- CNA just put up an article
- Great! I'll check it out.

Michael clicked off the television and brought his laptop into his bedroom where he pulled up the CNA site and read through the article once quickly. The list of Bishops participating was published at the end of the article and Michael noticed that the story did not specify why the Bishops would be heading to Rome in the first place.

Michael could hear the apartment door open and Justin and David speaking rapidly in the other room. He headed out to the living room to meet them.

"Hey guys," Michael said.

"Hey," Justin replied, walking into the kitchen with a large grocery bag.

"How's it going?" David asked, hanging his coat in the small front closet.

"Just fine. You guys have plans for the evening?" Michael asked.

"Just this funny movie," David told him, flashing a DVD case in his direction, "You got time to join us?"

"Yeah, I think I can. I need a break," Michael replied, sinking onto the sofa.

"Want some chicken wings and quesadillas?" Justin asked leaning out of the doorway of the kitchen and handing David a beer.

"You bet," David answered, snapping open the DVD case and putting the movie into the player.

"Sounds great," Michael agreed.

"I bought a two liter bottle of soda," Justin called to Michael, "want some?"

"Yeah, thanks."

Justin came out of the kitchen with a styrofoam container filled with chicken wings and a plastic cup full of soda for Michael. He put the container and the soda on the small table near the sofa and then returned to the kitchen for the container of quesadillas.

Michael relaxed into the sofa, munching on a quesadilla and listened to the guys debating about a project that David was working on at his office. The movie flicked on and Michael pushed the thoughts of what was happening in the parish of St. Monica's out of his mind.

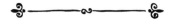

Monday morning, Michael arrived on campus to the buzz of talk about the Bishops being order to Rome. In between classes, pockets of seminarians and students stood around discussing the situation. The bishop that was Chancellor of the school had been one of those requested to attend.

At lunch time, Fr. Sullivan took a few minutes to request organized prayer and fasting for the week as a spiritual support to aid the Bishops.

"What do you think is going to happen?" Br. Jonathan asked the table once the rector had finished speaking.

Michael was sitting with his closest seminarian friends for lunch.

"Tis the beginning of another split," Michael suggested dramatically, smiling wryly.

Some of the seminarians chuckled without feeling.

"I was doing some research last night," Michael went on, "and it appears that the Pastor of St. Monica's is not the only priest in New England to make this suggestion in the name of furthering unity among the faiths."

"I agree with the split idea," said Br. Andrew nodding his head.

"Yeah, me too," agreed Br. Gregory.

Michael looked at them in surprise. He did not think they would take him seriously.

"Are you serious?" Michael asked.

Most of the heads around the lunch table bobbed their assent.

"But how long do you think before it happens?" he continued.

"I think that when these Bishops return, there will be some formalized discipline and then those who see this as a door to get out will find someone to rally behind and go," Br. Andrew explained.

"How will this affect the future of the Church here?" Michael asked with concern.

"Well, it could be pretty messy," Br. Gregory added. "Honestly, I believe that the bulk of the people won't understand what the fuss is about. They'll think — what's the big deal? Just give communion to everyone."

"Can you imagine?" Br. Jonathan asked rhetorically.

"I seriously can't believe that this is going on," Michael said again. "A few other friends of mine said they agreed with the split idea, but I thought that everyone was over-reacting."

"I don't know," Br. Gregory responded.

"Well, I've gotta get to my next class," Br. Andrew said as the group had lapsed into silence.

"Yeah me too," said Michael.

The guys stood up and gave thanks. Then they cleared up and went their separate ways for the remainder of the afternoon.

There was no news coming out of the meetings in Rome over the next few days. Michael attended his classes and really focused his attention on his school work. He tried to push the distraction of the meetings to the back of his mind. He spoke each day to Jessica who had been keeping in touch with Kelsey. He hadn't heard from Kelsey yet and he had thought about calling her. Every time he spoke with her, Jessica had counseled him to wait; when Kelsey was ready, she would call him herself.

Michael's phone rang just after dinner time on Thursday evening.

"Hey Michael." It was Kelsey.

"Hey Kels, how're you doing?" Michael asked. He wondered if she had gotten any news from the doctor.

"I'm doing alright," she told him, "Some days are better than others."

"I would imagine," he replied.

"I'm calling because I want to know if you know what's going on with the communion issue," Kelsey told him, "I spoke to one of the chaplains here today and he believes that more priests need to begin to behave like the Pastor at St. Monica's."

"I hope that you have access to another chaplain then," Michael said caustically.

"Yeah well, that's what I was thinking as well," Kelsey told him, "What do you think is going to come of this?"

"I believe in the end there will be some sort of formalized discipline. Folks around here seemed to agree that there might even be a split," he replied.

"How do you think it will affect the Church at large?"

"Well, besides promoting all sorts of misinformation on the Eucharist, I think in the end we will just end up with another new denomination," he told her. "I'm just not sure how long it will all take."

"How will we know where to go?" Kelsey asked concerned.

"Stick with priests that you know. I think it will be pretty clear in the short term who agrees with this Pastor and who does not," Michael advised.

"Yeah, I would imagine so," she agreed. "I didn't expect this would be an issue here where I am. I didn't know it was happening all around us."

"How's school going?" Michael asked changing the subject.

"Fine, I guess," she said.

Michael did not press her.

"The work is no problem," she told him, "It's just that I've been getting calls from girls all over campus who are having pregnancy concerns. It doesn't make any sense to me."

Michael nodded and thought of his father. To Kelsey he said, "Well, you have always been a natural leader."

"I just hope I'm telling them the right things," she lamented.

"Are you praying about it?" he asked.

"I try," she said, "sometimes everything happens so fast that I get overwhelmed."

"I understand," Michael told her.

"I always pray in the end," she said.

"Well, that's a good thing," he said.

"Yeah well, will you please call me if you hear anything more about the communion situation?" Kelsey asked.

"Sure, of course I will," Michael told her, "And Kels, try to take it easy."

"I know; I am," she said.

"I'll talk to you soon."

"Okay, thanks Michael. See you later."

Michael hung up the phone and decided to say a Rosary — first in Thanksgiving for Kelsey's new faith and also for the state of the Church in their area.

CHAPTER ELEVEN
The Strengthening

elsey did not call Michael or Anna regularly over the next few weeks. She began reporting in to Jessica and Hope instead. She made her way back and forth to the doctor's office a few times, following up on the hormone issues. In the end, Dr. Wilkes ordered an X-ray, the results of which had led to a second X-ray and a consultation with a couple of technicians.

Three more girls that Kelsey knew from college had also come forward to say that they thought they were pregnant. Word seemed to be making its way around that Kelsey was a great resource. She spent countless hours on campus speaking to any girl who found herself in a precarious situation.

It was early on a Wednesday morning when Kelsey's cell phone rang. She was still lying in bed, her alarm having just gone off. It was a number that she did not recognize. She answered it any way.

"Hello Kelsey, this is Adam," said the male voice flatly on the other end of the telephone.

"Hello Adam, how are you feeling today?" she asked with sincere concern.

Kelsey had forgotten that Adam had gone back to his parents' home to recover, that's why she didn't recognize the number. He had broken his right leg and his left wrist in the accident. Kelsey had gone to see him twice at the hospital. The first visit had gone pretty well since she had told him then that there was no baby. The second visit was a bit more awkward and strained.

"I feel like shit," he told her.

Kelsey raised her eyebrows but did not respond. There were a few minutes of silence on the other end of the phone.

"Can you come to the house to visit this weekend?" Adam asked suddenly.

"Adam, you know that you live too far away for me to come out," she told him. "It's a four hour drive."

"I miss you," he pleaded.

Kelsey took a deep breath. They had not discussed their relationship at all since the accident. The second time she stopped at the hospital, he had been really angry because she had gone back to her natural blond. She had also gained a couple of pounds. She looked better and she felt better. He had accused her of cheating on him with Michael. She knew he was hurt and angry, but it was also true that she was a different person — not one who was involved with Michael, but just different.

"You're like a different person," he complained again.

"Adam, you know that I care about you," she told him. "I pray for you every day."

He scoffed on the other end of the phone.

"And what's with that?" he accused. "I always thought you were too smart to fall for that organized religion crap?"

Kelsey took another deep breath. "You know what, Adam," she said finally, "I am a different person. I'm different than who I was before I thought that I was pregnant. I look at life differently now. I guess I've reorganized my priorities a bit."

He grumbled something unintelligible on the other end.

"You don't have to like it," she told him kindly.

"I don't!" he barked.

"Well, then what do you want to do about that?" she asked, feeling bad to challenge him, but tired of the pretense of keeping up with a relationship that no longer existed.

"I should just cut you loose," he threatened.

"Why don't you then?" she asked him.

"You wouldn't know what to do without me," he said condescendingly.

"You know what Adam," she replied, "I think you're onto something here... I think it's best if we take some time away from each other."

"Are you breaking up with me?" he asked her incredulously.

"No," she replied, "you're breaking up with me." She hoped that he could not hear her smile on the other end of the phone.

"I am?" he asked.

Kelsey felt badly for handling things this way, but she and Adam had been going at this for too long now. He called her often when his pain meds had taken affect. She knew that he was lashing out. She had never been able to determine if he had caused the accident on purpose, but in any event, it was clear that he blamed her for his predicament.

"Yes Adam, you are," she replied. "You've been saying it for some time now and I just haven't wanted to let it go. But you're right, it's time."

"Oh," he said on the other end. "Well good then; you need to get on with your life."

"And you, yours."

"When will I see you again?" he asked as if he were trying

to make sense of what this new arrangement would mean.

"I will always be your friend," Kelsey assured him. "And I'll see you when you get back to school."

"You're going to go out with that guy, Michael!" he accused thickly.

"This has nothing to do with Michael. Michael's just my friend," she told him sighing.

There was silence on the other end of the phone.

"Well Adam, take care of yourself. I hope you recover quickly," Kelsey said finally. "I'll keep praying for you."

"Whatever," he barked.

"Good-bye then."

"Bye."

Kelsey hung up the phone feeling just the slightest bit guilty. She had not intended to ever break up with Adam over the phone, but he had been withdrawn from the semester. He would be lucky to be up and around in time for the next one. He lived much too far away for her to ever get out there to see him in person and this antagonism between them would not be beneficial for his recovery.

She rolled over when she heard her dorm room open. Her roommate had just come back from the shower. She was fully dressed; just needing to grab her books. The two girls didn't spend much time together anymore. Things were strained between them as well. Kelsey could not wait for this semester to finally be over.

"Sorry, did I wake you?" her roommate asked.

"No, Adam did. He just called," she replied.

"How's he doing?"

"Not great. We just broke up," Kelsey explained.

"Broke up? Over the phone? That's harsh," her room mate accused, dumping the contents of her book bag onto her bed.

"Maybe, but it just wasn't working out any more. And it certainly was doing nothing good for Adam except distracting him from getting better."

Her roommate did not respond; she sorted books and notebooks from her bed and desk.

"Are you going away this weekend?" she asked finally, stuffing the last necessary notebook into the bag.

"Yeah, doctor's appointment," Kelsey told her.

"You're always going to the doctor now."

Kelsey did not respond. This was one appointment that she was not looking forward to. She had spoken to Dr. Wilkes yesterday and he wanted her to come back in. He had more concrete news for her. Just thinking about it made Kelsey's heart beat crazily.

"Well, I'll see you later then," her roommate said, pulling on her winter coat and slinging the bag over her shoulder.

"Okay, bye."

Kelsey sat up and pulled the covers tighter around her.

She grabbed her phone again and this time called Jessica, who she knew was already at work. She left a quick message saying that she had another appointment with the doctor and would need to stay at the house on Friday. Kelsey would drive out that way herself because she knew that Friday was Anna's Winter Formal. She tried to stop the pang of jealousy before it hit, but no luck.

Kelsey threw the covers back from her and stood, reaching quickly for her bathrobe. She grabbed her shower gear and headed down the hallway to the community bathroom. If there was any part of college that she hated, this was it. She wished that her college did not have dorms because then she could be in an apartment like Michael. She seemed to think of him constantly and she hated it.

When she got back to her room, there was a message on

her phone. She scowled — it was from Michael. She changed into a new pair of jeans and a long-sleeve sweater. She decided not to blow-dry her blonde hair, just pulled a brush though it quickly. She rooted around in her snack bin for a granola bar to eat for breakfast. She sat back on the bed, took a bite of the bar and pressed the voicemail button on her phone. Michael said that he wanted to take her to lunch on Saturday. He was calling to see if she would be up that way. She rolled her eyes and deleted the message. He was taking Anna to her Winter Formal the night before and he wanted to take her to lunch the next day. Would she ever get a handle on the idea that people could just be friends? She would figure out what to do about it later. Now, she needed to think about chemistry.

••••••••••••••••••○○••••••••••••••••••

Michael arrived at the Warner house at promptly five o'clock on Friday evening. He was wearing a tuxedo which made Lucy clap her hands in delight. He had spoken to Timothy about taking Anna out for dinner, as a surprise. Three of her friends were going with their dates to a small French restaurant downtown. Anna had mentioned it to Michael who had contacted Timothy and gotten his permission.

"Aren't you early?" asked Jane suspiciously, when she spied Michael standing in the living room in his tuxedo.

"Small surprise," he told her.

Jane smiled mischievously and went running up the stairs yelling loudly, "Anna!"

Lily led Anna down the stairs. Anna was wearing a lovely, long burgundy dress. It had long sleeves and black velvet applique on the skirt. She smiled shyly at Michael, who she thought looked stunning in a tuxedo.

He felt his face heat up and he looked away from her quickly so as not to stare. The modest dress made her look exquisite and he was honored to be her escort to the dance.

206

"What are you doing here already?" Anna asked, looking at her mother in confusion.

Lily stood to the side, smiling mysteriously.

Michael walked forward and handed Anna a small box with a wrist corsage in it.

"Well, we have dinner plans," he answered. "Did I forget to mention it?"

Anna's eyes widen in surprise as he slipped the flowers on her wrist. "What do you mean?"

"I mean we're going out with your friends to dinner at Jean Louis," he explained.

"Are you kidding?" Anna asked, looking from her mother to her father who had stepped into the living room from the dining room.

"No, he's not kidding," her father assured her. "And I'm even going to let him drive you. But you have to come back here for pictures before you go to the dance."

Anna smiled happily and ran to give her father a big hug. "Thanks, Daddy!"

Timothy smiled.

"Thank your mother," he told her with a twinkle in his eye, "She's the one who talked me into it."

Anna turned to hug her mom too.

"Have a nice time, honey," Lily said.

Michael took Anna's coat from Jane who had gotten it out of the front closet. Lily helped Anna to slide the wristlet off and back into the box.

Lucy stood on the bottom step, bouncing up and down with excitement.

"You look beautiful," she breathed to Anna. "Like a real princess."

"I agree," Michael told her.

"Why don't you leave the flowers here?" her mom

suggested. "You can get them when you return for pictures."

Anna nodded in agreement as Michael helped her into her coat. "The reservations are for 5:15," he told her, "So we need to get going."

"Thanks again," Anna said as she stepped into the front hall. All of her siblings had gathered on the stairs to see her go.

"Have fun," Jane said in a dreamy tone, thinking of the day when she might get to wear a dress like Anna's and have a date like Michael.

"The food is not so great there," Zack remarked off handedly.

"Zachariah!" Timothy said in annoyance, but everyone just laughed.

Michael helped Anna into the car and they waved as they backed out of the driveway. Anna saw her dad put an arm around her mom and she was grateful for such wonderful parents; even if she would never tell them that.

Dinner went by quickly. Michael seemed well at ease with Anna and her friends were very welcoming. They were a nice bunch.

"So are you going right to the dance?" Christian asked as they were standing to leave.

"No, we're going back to my house for pictures," Anna told him.

"Why don't you all come?" Michael suggested.

Anna gave him a warning look.

"Or maybe not... did you say all of your relatives were going to be there?" he asked quickly.

She bit her lip to keep from laughing.

"I think we'll pass," Christian said, "We'll just see you at the dance. We already did the picture thing at Jenny's."

"Yeah, we aren't going to come either, we have to go back to my house and get the tickets," Laura said as she and her date headed toward the door.

"I forgot them," Jack said sheepishly.

"And we're with them," Ashley remarked, glaring in Jack's direction.

The group walked out together and split up at the parking lot.

"What was that all about?" Michael asked as he and Anna headed in the direction of the car.

Anna did not reply.

"Please tell me this isn't still about the driving situation," Michael said.

Anna looked at him sheepishly.

"My friends are all so normal," she said, "And my parents are just so strict!"

Michael did not reply as he held the door for Anna. He noticed that none of the other guys did the same for their dates. Most of them were probably already being intimate. He could tell from the way they seemed to take one another for granted.

"I'm actually grateful your parents are so strict," Michael told her sliding into the seat.

Anna rolled her eyes.

"It saves me from having to do all the hard work myself," he finished. "You might think I'm strange, but it's hard work being alone with a girl as beautiful as you and trying to do the right thing all the time."

She looked at him sideways, but didn't respond. He glanced in her direction and he could see her cheeks aflame with color.

Michael and Anna arrived back at the house for photos. In the interim, Jessica and Hope had come by with the girls and Stephen. Everyone was talking and laughing at once and then every person in the house had to have an individual picture taken with Anna and Michael. Anna was thankful that she and Michael were such good friends. Any other guy who had had to be exposed to this type of situation would be long gone by morning!

The two left shortly after pictures, being chauffeured by Timothy to the High School gym. The dance was an enormous success. Both Michael and Anna had a great time and they were surprised when the night had come quickly to an end. The Warner house was empty and quiet when Timothy returned them to the doorstep, just after midnight. Michael stayed for a cup of coffee but then he headed home as well since he was not able to get the next day off from work.

Michael got a text from Jessica early Saturday morning while he was at work. It was a request for prayers for Kelsey. She had had a pretty restless night. Michael knew that she was heading to see the doctor again. He prayed that this time they would have something more concrete to tell her. He had hoped to meet Kelsey for lunch, but she had said that she would need to call him after the appointment.

Michael left work at noon and still had not heard from Kelsey. He went back to his apartment to work on school stuff. At two o'clock, he finally gave in and made himself a sandwich. Even if Kelsey called right then it would still be an hour before they could meet. He sent a text to Jessica at two thirty.

- Things okay over there?
- Not great, no. She wants to see u 2morrow.
- Whatever she wants.
- Call you later xo

Michael grabbed his coat and headed out to the Adoration chapel to say a few prayers for Kelsey. He ran into some of the guys from the seminary there and he asked them to pray for her as well. On his way to the grocery store, he called Anna.

"Hey, how are things?" Michael asked, when she picked

up.

"Mainly good," she replied.

"Kelsey had another appointment," he told her.

"Yeah, I know, she called me," Anna said.

"When?"

"About an hour ago."

"Oh," he said.

"I'm guessing you haven't talked to her yet," Anna said.

"No, she wants to see me tomorrow," Michael explained.

"That's good. I'm happy she wants to see you."

Michael nodded his head, but refrained from asking the question that he wanted to. Instead he asked, "Did you have a nice time yesterday?"

"I did," she told him, "Thank you so much for going with me."

He smiled. "It was my pleasure."

"And did I ever really thank you for setting up the dinner arrangements? That was so great," she said.

"You're welcome," he replied.

"How do you feel about proms?" she asked laughing.

He paused a half-second, smiling.

"Let me know when it is and I'll see if it works in my schedule," he told her, "but I don't know if my parents will let me stay out all night at your overnight party."

They laughed together.

"But really, I'm hoping to travel this spring, so if you're serious, let me know soon and I'll see if I'm going to be in town," he explained.

"Oh," she said, "Where are you going?"

"I want to go on a mission trip," he replied. "I just don't know if I'll be able to afford it."

"Haiti?" she asked.

"Yeah, we'll see."

"I'll pray," she offered.

"That would be great," he told her.

"Take care, Michael," she said.

"You too, Anna."

He hung up as he drove into the parking lot, wondering about proms and Kelsey and how he would find enough money to be able to go on the Haiti mission trip that he was interested in.

·············•••●•••·············

When Michael returned to his apartment complex an hour later, with a bag full of groceries and two movies, he was surprised to find Kelsey's car in the spot next to the sidewalk. He got out of his car quickly and went over to her vehicle on the driver's side. Her head was leaning on her arms which were crossed over the steering wheel. Michael knew it was really bad before he even knocked on her window. He noticed that she had gone back to her natural blonde and he smiled sadly. He took a deep breath and knocked softly. Kelsey looked up at him with tears streaked all down her face. He opened her door and knelt down near the driver's seat.

"I hope you didn't drive like that," he scolded gently.

When she did not respond, he put his hand under her arm and applied a small amount of pressure. She automatically got out of the car. Michael shut her door and then opened his passenger side to grab the groceries and movies then steered Kelsey toward the apartment. She remained quiet during their walk up the flight of stairs and into his place. His roommates still were not home but there had been a message from one of them on his cell while he was talking to Anna. He would check it later. He steered Kelsey onto the couch and he left her a moment to put the groceries in the small kitchen.

When he came back around the corner, Kelsey had curled her arms around her bent knees and was sobbing. Michael rushed over to her side and put his arms around her. She stayed stiff in his embrace and he relaxed his hold, not wanting to make her uncomfortable.

"Kels, you can talk to me," he whispered gently.

She bowed her head on her knees and wailed with a grief so keen that it made the hair on the back of Michael's neck stand up. He immediately let go of her and began instead to rub her back.

"Kels, please, tell me what's going on," he begged her quietly, rubbing her back steadily. "I want to be able to help you."

"No one can help me now," she wailed. She looked at him intently. "I want to die."

Michael continued to rub her back and with his other hand he started rubbing her lower leg. He wondered for a moment if Adam had died and if Kelsey felt responsible.

"Kelsey, I know that it's bad. I know that it seems like it will be bad forever," he said softly.

"My life is over, Michael," she sobbed.

He did not respond other than to bow his head over hers.

In a few minutes she was all cried out. He lifted his head when he sensed that she wanted to look at him. Her eyes held a grief so deep that he felt complete despair. She turned and looked out past him into nothingness. He whispered a prayer to St. Michael.

"Can you talk to me, Kels?" he asked her softly. "Can you tell me what's going on?"

"I went back to the doctor," she said flatly.

He did not respond.

"He told me that…" She shuddered suddenly and he held her tightly.

"He told me," she began again, "that I will never be able to have children."

Kelsey bowed her head and began to sob anew.

Michael held her tightly as his own eyes filled with tears.

"I am so sorry," he whispered, as the tears slid down his own cheeks. "I'm so sorry, Kelsey."

The two of them sat crying on the couch for the next few minutes.

"I don't understand," she whispered. "Why would God do this?"

Michael did not speak. Sometimes grief was not the right time to debate theology.

"No one will ever want me," she breathed. "No man will ever want a wife who can't have babies. I want to be dead."

This time Michael was the one who shuddered.

"Kelsey, I know that you won't believe this now, but God still has a plan for you," he said softly.

"What kind of plan could he possibly have for me?"

Michael could not answer that question. "It doesn't make a lick of sense," he said instead, "but the strength of God will get you through this."

He thought for a few moments of the last few weeks of Kelsey's life journey and was able to see the way that God had called her back to himself before she would need him in the most difficult moments of her life.

"Doesn't he know that I'm sorry?" she asked Michael suddenly, desperately. "Doesn't he know that I'm sorry for having slept with Adam, for dying my hair, for trying to be someone I'm not? Didn't he care that I tried to come back?"

Michael listened to her desperate questions and just pulled her into a huge hug.

"You didn't do this, Kelsey," he told her, holding her tightly.

"It's not fair!" she yelled, horse from sobbing. "I came back; I told him I was sorry, I even meant it!"

Kelsey pushed away from Michael angrily.

"And Adam… he's just fine!" she spat, getting to her feet and beginning to pace in Michael's small living room.

Michael watched her sadly. He knew she would need to go through all of the stages of grief and the next few weeks and months, even years, would be a difficult time for her. He wished that he could take some of that pain away, but he knew he couldn't.

"Adam and I broke up," Kelsey said still pacing.

"I think that is good for you." Michael chanced a reply.

Kelsey stopped right where she was and she spun to face Michael. "What difference does that make?" she demanded.

"Who have you talked to about this?" Michael asked instead. "Jessica and Hope?"

Kelsey stood where she was and nodded.

"What was their counsel?" he asked.

She sank to the floor and pulled her knees back up to her chest. The pain that she was experiencing was so profound that she winced.

"Kels, what did they say?" he prodded gently.

"They said they would pray a novena to St. Jude," she whispered.

Michael stood up to cross to where Kelsey sat, but she held him back with her hand. She did not want to be comforted right then.

"They said I should pray, they said I should speak to Fr. Gregory Mary, I should go to adoration, I should read the psalms…"

Michael nodded his head as she looked at him.

"I can't!" She struggled to breathe. "I can't! I can't!"

Michael went to her anyway as she started to cry again. He held her close as she continued to cry. After a few minutes, he helped her up and directed her to the couch. She curled up

215

facing away from him and Michael sat on the floor rubbing her back. In minutes, she was asleep.

Michael took a deep breath and leaned back against the edge of the couch. He blew the breath out and looked at Kelsey's sleeping form. She looked so much better than the last time he had seen her — back to her natural hair color and she had put on a few pounds. His eyes filled with tears again for her grief and he bowed his head and prayed silently.

He got up quietly and grabbed the quilt from the back of the couch. He lowered it gently onto Kelsey. He kissed the top of her head and went quietly into his room. The first thing he did was to call Jessica.

"She's there?" Jessica asked without even saying hello.

"How could you have even let her drive here?" Michael demanded.

"What could we do? We couldn't get her keys away from her?" Jessica replied. "Hope followed her all the way to the highway, but came back because she was afraid that Kelsey would go too fast to try to get away from her."

Michael did not respond. He sank onto his bed and rested his elbows on his knees.

"Michael, you okay?" Jessica asked after a minute.

"Yeah." He cleared his throat. Jessica knew he had been crying as well.

"How is she now?" Jessica asked gently.

"Sleeping," he responded.

"Do you want me to come over? Send Hope? What can we do?" she asked. "Martha's back. Kelsey's met her and she'll come too if you need her."

"I don't know," Michael said, running his free hand over his short, dark hair and sighing. "Maybe it's better that she just stay here and get some sleep into her."

"Well, you call us if you need anything, any time, okay?"

Jessica asked.

"Yeah, I will," he promised. "I'm sorry I was short with you."

"I love you, Michael," Jessica said.

Michael hung up from the call and checked his messages. Justin had sent a note saying that they would be spending the night up at the wedding instead of driving back the same day. Michael erased the message and sent a quick one out to Anna asking for prayers for Kelsey. Anna's response came quick:

- Already praying.
- J, H, M & I r beginning a novena to St. Jude.
- Ok; on it. U ok?
- Maybe
- Is she w/u?
- Yeah - fell asleep.
- Call if u need 2 talk
- Thx

Michael checked the time. It was just about ten. He went out to check on Kelsey who was still sleeping. He left a light on in the kitchen in case she woke during the night. He did not want her to be disoriented. He changed quickly and slipped under his covers. He got up suddenly and did something that he had never done before — locked his bedroom door. He did not think he could handle another scene tonight and would have hated it if Kelsey had just walked into his bedroom.

Michael woke up early Sunday morning. He knew when he did that Kelsey was already gone. He lay in bed for a few minutes and then decided he had better check for sure. She was no longer on the couch when he walked down the hallway and the apartment was empty of anyone but himself. He checked the kitchen counter for a note, but nothing had been left there. He sank onto the couch and ran a hand through his hair. He just sat there for a short while, doing nothing but thinking about everything that Kelsey was going through. He prayed a moment for her safety. He did not know what her frame of mind was when she left; he hoped that God would protect her from herself.

He considered his options for the morning and decided to go first to the adoration chapel. He showered and dressed quickly. As he walked toward his car, he scanned the parking lot to see if Kelsey had returned, but her car was not there.

The drive to the small chapel was fairly quick. Michael was astonished to see Kelsey's car in the lot along with another vehicle he did not recognize. He sat in his car in the parking lot and debated whether or not to go inside. He decided to wait for the time being. He did not want to disturb Kelsey in her prayer. He drove instead to a small coffee shop down the road. He parked facing the road to watch if Kelsey drove past and began reciting a rosary for her.

Michael's phone rang just as he was finishing the final prayer.

"Hey," Kelsey said quietly. "You went out."

"Yeah, I noticed you were gone. I'm at a local coffee shop," he replied. "Are you back at the apartment?"

"Yeah, I just got back," she said.

He did not ask where she had gone and she did not offer any further information.

"Do you want me to bring you coffee back?" he asked.

"That would be great. I'm sorry to have caused all this chaos in your life," she told him.

"It's no trouble, Kelsey. I'd be lying if I said I wasn't worried about you, but I worry about all of my friends," he explained. "What do you want for coffee?"

"Just a regular one," she replied.

"There's a key under the mat that the planter is sitting on; if you want to let yourself in," he told her.

"No, I'd rather wait for you," she replied. "I think I'd feel weird walking around your empty apartment."

"Be back soon," he said.

"Drive safe," she told him.

He chuckled. "Yeah, like you should be giving driving advice."

They both laughed softly and hung up the line.

Kelsey was leaning up against her car talking on her cell when Michael drove back into the parking lot. The winter wind was wiping her long blonde locks around. She looked tired, but not distraught. He exited the car with a tray and two coffees on it. He stayed on his side of the vehicle to give Kelsey some space in her phone conversation. She motioned him to go ahead and she followed him up the stairs. She clicked her phone shut just as he was letting her into the house.

They both walked over to the table and sat down. Michael pulled out Kelsey's coffee and set it down in front of her.

"How are you doing this morning?" he asked.

She nodded her head. "Some better than yesterday," she replied. "I went to the adoration chapel."

Michael took a sip of coffee.

"I'm still pretty mad," Kelsey confessed.

"That's okay, Kelsey," he assured her, "All of that isn't going to go away overnight. Or even with a visit or two to the adoration chapel."

"My doctor thinks there's a big picture situation going on here," she told him.

"What do you mean?"

Kelsey raised her eyebrows, which were also blonde again. "Well, he's been speaking with a scientist…it seems I'm not the only girl in this kind of circumstance," she explained.

Michael nodded.

"Is that your dad?" she asked.

"Yeah," he confessed.

"Do you know what their theories are?" she asked him, looking down.

"No, Kelsey. I don't know. I swear!" he exclaimed.

She looked up at him.

"Honestly," he said.

She nodded, but didn't offer any more information.

"What are you going to do now?" he asked.

"Well, today I'm going to go to Mass. I think I'm going to go alone though — if you don't mind. I don't need an audience to my scene."

"Of course," he told her.

"Then I'm going to go back to school and try to set my mind on something other than this for a while," she finished.

He did not respond.

"Yes, I've also put a call in to Fr. Gregory Mary," she told him, answering the unasked question.

"Is there anything I can do?" Michael asked her.

"If you could pray the St. Jude novena with Jessica, Hope, and the others, I would greatly appreciate that," Kelsey replied.

"Of course," he said. "Will you call me soon? Just to check in?"

Kelsey nodded.

"I don't want to be overbearing, Kels," he told her.

"You've been an amazing friend, Michael," she replied. "I truly appreciate your concern and I promise to make it a priority to keep in touch."

They drank their coffees in silence.

"Someday, after I understand what really went on here, I'd like to talk to people about all this," Kelsey said.

Michael regarded her cautiously.

"Seriously," she said.

"That would be an amazing gift for you to give the world,

Kelsey," he said.

"It'll be a good long while though," she said.

"Better late than never," he remarked softly.

They both smiled.

"Well, I'm gonna get outta here," she said standing.

Michael stood as well. He went over and pulled Kelsey into another huge hug.

"I love you Kelsey, you are an amazing person," he whispered.

She drew back and looked at him, her hazel eyes glistening with tears.

"I'm not amazing at all," she protested. "Just all sorts of messed up."

"Think what you want," he said, "I know better."

"Thank you so much for your friendship, Michael," she said.

He wiped the falling tear from her cheek and gave her another squeeze.

"I really will keep in touch," she assured him.

"I know you will," he said. "Be careful driving home."

Kelsey walked in the direction of the door.

"And Kels, don't forget about all the other people who love you," he reminded her gently.

"I know," she said. "I've got to do something about my parents. I'm not quite ready yet."

He held her gaze.

"Pray for me," she said.

"I will."

Michael watched as Kelsey shut the door quietly behind her.

EPILOGUE

Kelsey's phone rang late on the Thursday night before the last week of the semester. She did not recognize the number, but considering that she often did not these days, she answered any way.

"I'm calling for Kelsey," said a shy voice on the other end.

"This is Kelsey," she replied.

"Kelsey, you don't know me, but I'm Amanda," the girl said by way of an introduction.

"Hi Amanda," Kelsey said gently.

Amanda began to weep quietly on the other end of the phone. "I'm really scared," she said.

"Are you on-campus?" Kelsey asked her gently.

"Um-hum."

"Do you want to meet?" Kelsey asked.

"It's late; I don't want to drag you out. And it's cold," Amanda said, sniffing loudly.

"Where are you?" Kelsey asked.

"I'm on the other side of campus from you," Amanda answered.

Kelsey checked her watch. "There will be another campus shuttle in fifteen minutes." She knew the schedule by heart now. "I can be at your dorm in twenty-five minutes."

"Are you sure?" Amanda asked.

"I'll leave right now," Kelsey told her, getting out of bed and grabbing her heavy coat from the hook on the door.

"Thanks Kelsey," Amanda said, crying openly again on the other end of the phone.

Kelsey made her way up to Amanda's dorm room and knocked quietly on the door. She had no trouble these days getting into the dorms at any hour of the day or night. The Resident Advisors all knew who she was and why she was there.

Kelsey knew it was Amanda at the door because the girl began sobbing as soon as she opened it. Kelsey stepped into the room and shut the door behind her. She shrugged out of her heavy coat quickly and let it drop to the floor. She whispered the St. Michael prayer quietly and just held Amanda as she cried.

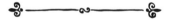

Patrick, Michael's father, and Kelsey met up at the same coffee shop in Carlstown that she and Michael often went to. Patrick hugged Kelsey tightly when she made her way over to the table that he had been sitting at.

"Hello Kelsey," he said in his gruff voice. Patrick was a handsome looking older man. Kelsey could see from looking at him where Michael got his good looks. Patrick had filled out with age, but she could still see the athletic build of the guy he once was.

"Hello, Mr. Anderson," she replied.

"It's so good of you to agree to see me again," he told her.

"I'm happy to help. It makes me feel like I'm doing something useful," she said, taking the seat across from him.

Patrick studied her intently. He was happy that she had gone back to her natural blonde and had added a few pounds. She looked a bit more lean and muscular. He hoped that she had taken his advice and joined a gym.

Kelsey pulled a notebook out of her shoulder bag and flipped it open. Placing it on the table, she took a sip from the mug of coffee that he had ordered for her.

"It looks like the count is up to thirty-seven," she told him.

He nodded, tight-lipped.

"And we all arrived at the school at about the same time last year," she continued.

"Any news on the good doctor?" Patrick asked, caustically.

Kelsey shook her head. "No one knows where he went. Any news on your end?"

Patrick looked at her sadly. "Well, the map is beginning to be taken over by pushpins. The problem is there are clusters all over the country."

Kelsey looked away.

"How's Michael?" she asked to change the subject.

"He's doing well. He's out of school soon, but he'll be staying at his apartment over break this year. I hope to see him at Christmas." Patrick told her. "When does your Winter break start?"

"Next week," she replied. "My finals are over December 8th."

"I think then, you should give this up for a bit," he waved at her notebook, "and make sure to get your course work taken care of."

Kelsey nodded and sighed resignedly. She put her chin in her hand and watched Patrick typing quickly on his laptop.

"What if we plan to meet next at my office, after the first of the year? I can show you some of the information that we have collected and catalogued," he bribed, "as long as you pass your finals okay?"

"That would be great!" she exclaimed. "Would you really

show me that kind of information?"

"If you are part of the research staff then you are entitled to it. My colleagues and I have been talking to girls like you all around the country. We've done all of this work word-of-mouth. I think we need to bring someone like you on-board. Are you interested in an internship over break?"

Kelsey nodded thoughtfully.

"I'll call you the first week of January," Patrick said, signing off and closing his laptop.

"That sounds great," she agreed.

"Try and have a nice holiday, Kelsey," Patrick told her, patting her hand which was resting on the notebook open on the table.

She nodded and moved to pull out her laptop as he stood to leave. He leaned over and gave her a kiss on the forehead.

"School work," he reminded her. "The research will still be there after your finals."

Here ends the first book of the *Kelsey's Journey* series. The next book will be called *Confession*.

Crisis Pregnancy Resources

Sisters of Life
~ pregnancy resources, healing after abortion, retreats for women
- In the United States: 877-777-1277 (toll free)
- In Canada: 877-543-3380 (toll free)
- On the Web: www.sistersoflife.org

Priests for Life
~ pregnancy resources, healing after abortion, clergy resources
- Toll Free: 888-735-3448
- On the Web: http://www.priestsforlife.org/pregnant-need-help/index.aspx

Option Line
~ pregnancy resources, emergency contraception information, abortion information
Note: Option Line and our network of participating pregnancy centers offers peer counseling and accurate information about all pregnancy options; however, these centers do not offer or refer for abortion services or the morning-after pill.
- Toll Free: 800-712-HELP
- On the Web: http://www.optionline.org/

Find a Crisis Pregnancy Center Near You
The life-affirming organizations listed do not refer for or promote abortion. Alternative services and accurate information about abortion are provided free of charge.
- On the Web: http://findpregnancyhelp.com/

Society of the Body of Christ
Sister Anne Sophie
234 Rossiter
Corpus Christi, Texas, 78411-1450
361-814-768
savesoul@swbell.net

22526300R00130

Made in the USA
Middletown, DE
03 August 2015